JEWELS FROM MY POCKET

JEWELS FROM MY POCKET

Stewart B Powell

August 19, 2004

To Frank and June —

No more missed hair appointments?

iUniverse, Inc.
New York Lincoln Shanghai

Jewels from my Pocket

iUniverse, Inc.

For information address:
iUniverse, Inc.
2021 Pine Lake Road, Suite 100
Lincoln, NE 68512
www.iuniverse.com

Final copy edit by iUniverse

Cover art by Douglas Thayer

ISBN: 0-595-32112-7

Printed in the United States of America

For Deborah

With special thanks to Margo Kielhorn for her editorial skills

CONTENTS

▼

1975: THE GREETING

The new malls proudly represent the shopping meccas of the future. Their sleek, contemporary structures boast August-like heat in January and October-like briskness in the sweltering, humid Michigan summer days—truly a marvel to weather-beaten shoppers. Here I was, bumping down the sidewalk from the bus terminal in downtown Pershing, now a decaying shadow of the majesty it once held. Abandoned by urban sprawl, Pershing was no different from other downtown districts across the country attempting to compete with those architecturally amazing coliseums of shopping pleasure in the suburbs.

No matter—my summer employment "opportunity" was only a temporary "fix" intended to develop my nonexistent work ethic. No summer vacation for me. With my parents nipping at my heels, insisting that I earn some of my own keep, Uncle Dale told them I could be put to good use in his jewelry shop. So I walked down the crumbling sidewalk, passing the majestically carved sandstone facade of the old Pershing Theater, a landmark now closed and silent but the source of cherished memories for many local folks. I hadn't been by here for years—not since the megatheaters opened at the malls. We could take dates there and see any of four movies, depending on our mood, without having to watch the childish cartoon at the beginning. I must confess that as I strode past the grand structure, I had a new appreciation for its beauty and size. Still intact, the marquis appeared ready to light the entire street if someone switched on the breaker.

At the "ripe" age of seventeen, the fragility of my fleeting youth was palpable. I could almost smell the popcorn with *real* butter—not that yellow grease they use now—and visualize the velvet curtain rising gracefully as the lights dimmed, and I could almost hear the sound of animated characters echoing through the huge hall. Nah, who should care? The biggest department store in the city still held its ground here and the best restaurants around kept this small metropolis humming. Certainly these realities wouldn't change for a long time; the new shopping centers were the future. I would stick around here a bit to watch this place crumble…just a little more.

Clay's Department Store was just down the block from Uncle Dale's shop, looming on the next corner in its full art deco style, a giant yellow and blue enameled building right out of *Modern Science* magazine. I shuffled up to the building and turned the corner. Walking up the side street, I passed swarms of clerks, wrappers, maintenance crews, and operators arriving to take their stations at Clay's, chattering and giggling at the start of a new day. Contagious smiles were all around. These people actually seemed to look forward to their work ahead. I stumbled past, gawking in the windows at all the smiling people, as I was oddly surprised by their pleasantness. I had always imagined that people worked out of duty alone, not that they derived pleasure from it.

My destination lay next door in a dwarfed little brick building, attached to Clay's but very different architecturally. Even the shop's black enameled panels under the storefront windows seemed to say, "Look at me, I fit right in with 'Big Yeller.'" The building looked older…much older, and seemed stalled in history. Most other buildings in downtown Pershing had been remodeled, rather like those in Old West movie streetscapes that had a great elaborate front, but nothing behind except long two-by-four props to hold them up. In our downtown, however, these facades were supported by dirty old brick buildings with long forgotten names and dates embossed into the stone, hidden from the world like embarrassing birthmarks. The birthmarks on this building were still evident in the sandstone ledges across the pediment, the window ledges, and the big sign that proudly shouted "Wynn & Scutter Jewelers." This was my destination.

The structure had to be older than pavement. I'd seen pictures of the original downtown, complete with dirt roads. Horses, mules, wagons, and worn leather boots provided the transport of the day, and I have no doubt that if a photographer had aimed his trusty camera in this direction, he would have captured a still of the proud "Wynn & Scutter Jewelers" sign in its prime. Still quite serviceable now, the sign is easy to read. The ancient dinosaur still attracts attention; it certainly attracted mine with its old steel cables, rusty now, just a shadow of the shiny coiled ropes they had been.

The clock juxtaposed at the end of the sign read 8:35 a.m. as the sun gently struck the pavement and sidewalks on the other side of the street, but I could see from the tall buildings' outcroppings that this little shop window was destined to remain forever in the shade. Occupying most of the entrance, the shop windows stood empty, save for a few clocks hanging from the rough wood backboard. Below the clocks, the waist-high window displays brightened up and enhanced the otherwise distinguished atmosphere within. The deep royal blue, bright red, and royal purple satin displays glowed even in the shade, somehow, as if reaching for the sunlight beyond their grasp.

Flanked by the dazzling windows, the shop door beckoned me through the gently-inclining, ever-narrowing cream and pale green mosaic tile entryway. A huge air-conditioning unit was suspended by cables that mimicked those on the sign, yet they appeared less sturdy. Perhaps my tendency to arrive early was not such a godsend after all. I was not expected till 9:00 a.m. Apparently, neither was anyone else. If I had been worried about my first day of employment before, the flutters definitely welled up in my belly now as I waited nervously.

I held my ground at the door. Bashful throughout my youth, I knew that walking away was out of the question, as my return would surely have been doubtful. Most of my previous summers had been spent in blissful freedom in northern Michigan at my grandmother's lakeside cottage with numerous and ever-changing friends. I had always felt the good life would continue endlessly, but my parents, generous as they are, clearly felt it was time to introduce responsibility into my life.

So this was it. I expected Uncle Dale to be the first to brighten the doorstep, as this was his shop. My uncle, Dale Hammond, had joined the family only a few years before when Aunt Lilly finally snagged the man of her dreams. We thought it would never happen.

Daydreaming now about the dismal prospects of my summer, I was startled back into reality by the sound of Aunt Lilly's version of my own name.

"Stevie—you've gotta be him! You're early, but we'll excuse it this time." The voice continued from behind me, "Hi, I'm Mick. Welcome to the Big D's place."

I shook hands with a gangly, youthful man I pegged at about 25 years of age, who sported the fashion of the day: a brightly-colored print shirt, bell-bottom slacks, and just the kind of wide leather belt with a double row of holes that I wanted. The wide tie loosely knotted around Mick's neck didn't look like a comfortable addition to the ensemble, but I knew it was one of Uncle Dale's requirements. Mick's most impressive feature was his Fu-Man-Chu mustache that dangled below a pair of huge tortoise shell eyeglasses. Over the years I had seen my share of mustaches—handlebars, traditional, with and without goatees, full beards, you name it—but this was something the likes of which I had never seen in the "real" world. Shoulder-length blonde hair topped off Mick's very "with-it" look. At that instant it seemed the "real world" was quite different from the world I called my own."We'll get her opened up and I'll show you around," offered Mick. "Don't say anything you wouldn't want anyone else to hear, because I've got to check in with security when we go in. They'll be able to hear every word we say until the burglar alarm is shut down; they can probably hear us now."

Mick opened the aluminum and glass door and I realized it didn't fit in with the exterior architecture; it fit this scene like auto-pilot on the Santa Maria. The ring of a brass bell sounded as the door swung open and we stepped into the dark interior.

"Sure am glad the Big D had that new door installed. Couldn't see a thing coming in here with the old wood slab that was there before. Nice not havin' to carry a flashlight. Hang on."

Mick swung open a tiny gate between the glass counters to the left of us and stepped behind them. I stood still as he threaded his way through the dim light to a dark archway at the back of the room where he lifted the receiver off the phone. "Howdy! This is 18–7–7…Everything's fine…Yeah, we're ready to go…Yep he's the boss's nephew…We're okay."

"Hey, man, I'll shed some light on the subject so you can have a look," Mick said as he disappeared around a corner.

I stood nervously, afraid to move in any direction. Only moments passed before lights began to flicker above my head and row after row of lights snapped on to reveal glitter-filled showcases reflecting everywhere. Archways to different rooms appeared, ceilings soared above me some 15 feet, and the ornate stampings on the tin gave way to floral patterned olive green wallpaper that complemented the equally green carpet. The shop was fully furnished in wood—maple, oak, walnut—and glass; nothing seemed to match, yet everything blended together, accented by the glisten and shine of gold and silver throughout.

Only when the door swung open behind me and the brass bell—louder inside—rang to announce an arrival did I realize I had been holding my breath. I unglued my feet from the spot where I stood, transfixed. I turned to watch a thin, slight man, whose lack of stature was accentuated by slightly stooping shoulders, whisk through the door.

"Whatsa matter, cat got yer tongue?" he grumbled, nearly trailing his open trench coat on the floor, "Yer pretty jumpy for a fella shopping before breakfast. We don't open for 45 minutes, ya know."

"Mornin,' Sherm!" chirped Mick, saving the moment as he came back around the corner, because surely the cat did have my tongue.

"You've got a flounder out here," Sherm said as his eyes blinked through his wire-rimmed glasses, his face drawn and stern. "He don't talk much, either," Sherm reported as he breezed by me and through the tiny gate between the show-cases, his coattails barely keeping up as they followed him around the same corner Mick had just rounded.

Mick laughed and looked back. "This is Stevie, Big D's nephew. We've got a new one to break in, Sherm."

"This will be a fun one. He can't even talk," Sherm's muffled voice called out from the back room. Already nervous, I wished I hadn't eaten breakfast.

As Mick took a step forward and leaned on a glass counter, my eyes focused as the glitter faded, and I could count five maple-and-glass showcases, each measuring about six feet long, flanking the shop's center aisle. They formed a "U" configuration with the massive oak case at the end of the room where Mick was standing. Two freestanding smaller cases appeared as islands, breaking up the center of the shop. My interrupted image reflected back at me from mirrored wall cases filled with blue satin boxes containing pearls and stones of every color, silver trays and teapots, clocks, watches, and wood jewelry boxes. Glittering gold crafted into every conceivable shape was displayed throughout, and here I was—the proverbial bull in the china shop. Not only was this creature out of his familiar environment, but he couldn't talk, either.

"Don't worry about Sherm," Mick said. "He'll grow on ya as long as you don't mess with his stuff."

A little time to absorb the last few minutes would have provided welcome relief. Perhaps my breakfast would settle back into its happy place and my vocal chords would reconnect with my brain. It was not to be, however. Time was not on my side when, like the striking of a clock, the doorbell rang out again. "Ding, clank…ding, clank." I realized now that the bell rang surely enough on its first swing, but the heavy brass clanked back on the glass with its return.

The first "ding, clank" brought a laugh, followed by a lady. The laugh was a raspy, wide-mouthed, happy kind of sound you knew would be followed by a smile. Behind the laugh came a slender, attractive, middle-aged woman. The laugh, which resolved into the smile I expected, was accompanied by a slightly startled look—the kind you might receive when caught eavesdropping. "Good morning," said the lady through her smile.

With my neurotransmitters fully functional again, I had barely uttered, "Good…" when a chipper but demanding voice cried out, "Keep it movin'! You know this is a no parking zone!" from behind the slowly approaching lady.

"Hi ya, Molly," Mick jumped in, as if on cue. "You're actually on time this morning. What gives?" he kidded with a loud chuckle.

"Well," the lady responded with a rasp, "Billy and I started gabbin' when we met at the corner, so I just had to say 'no' to the girls for coffee this morning."

At the callow age of 17, I was completely unfamiliar with the type of merchandise one would purchase at this store. I had never been here before and I had no idea with whom or how many people I would be working. Any jewelry stores I had accidentally wandered into had been staffed by astute-looking salespeople dressed in business apparel. So far, no one at Wynn & Scutter matched that description. Molly, dressed in slacks and a sweater and coiffed with the biggest, immobile ball of wavy, permed, red hair I had ever seen, oozed with gold and diamonds. Dripping with as much jewelry on her person as the showcases around me, Molly vacated the aforementioned "no parking zone" to make room for the man behind her.

Taking it all in thus far, we had a fella who looked like a 60s fashion plate, a man who looked like my dentist when he was proudly grinding a volcanic crater into my tooth, a dead ringer for a lonely rich widow on a daytime soap opera, and another arrival.

"Hi, I'm Bill," the newcomer said as he offered a handshake. "You're Steve, I'll wager."

"Don't bother, Bill," Sherm's voice came from behind me. I cranked my beet-colored face around to see him leaning on the counter next to Mick. "He can't talk—not even a grunt, poor thing."

I felt a hand on my arm, and as Molly warmly said "Don't pay any attention to the ole geezer, Steve," she threw Sherm a ferocious glance.

"Good morning," I finally squeaked out to Molly. I was on a roll now, but as I went for the finish line, "Hi, Bill…"my greeting was interrupted.

"Oh, God. He *can* talk!" snapped Sherm from behind me as he turned and walked to the back again. "Yep, it's worse than I thought."

Obviously sadists, the other three laughed.

*   *   *   *

Bill was as different from the rest as they were different from each other. He wore a blue topcoat buttoned all the way to his chin, a touring cap pulled down to his ears and he carried an umbrella that dangled just above a pair of heavy black leather shoes, the kind service station attendants wear during the cold winter months. In mid-June, I figured he must be cooking his morning eggs under that heavy coat and a bead of sweat formed on my brow just at the thought.

"Billy, why don't you take off your coat and stay a while?" chimed Mick.

"Awe, hush. I'm just warming myself up before you turn on this infernal air conditioning machine and chill this place off like a packing house again."

Bill obviously didn't care much for air-conditioned comfort. You might think a person with such an affinity for warmth would allow some natural insulation to grow on his head at a time when even the staunchest conservative wouldn't be caught dead with the tops of his ears showing. But here was Bill, thick black eye-glass frames, pure whitewalls, and a five o'clock shadow adorning his now hatless head.

"Dale won't be in for another half-hour, so you might as well let us get you settled in," Molly said as Mick offered, "Come on back and I'll show you some things you'll need to know."

Molly disappeared instantly to attend to her work. Bill on the other hand, was slow and calculating in his movements. He gestured for me to follow, and I finally made it past the tiny gate. Sherm or no Sherm, I had to go back there.

The backs of the console showcases betrayed their age; each featured six large drawers below the display platform, and they all showed signs of having been kicked, scratched, gouged, slammed, and overstuffed since, I figured, sometime around the Napoleonic era. The wall cases were a pure work of art. A veritable collage of wood and ingenuity, a painted plywood shelf unit separated two large factory-built cases. Walls above the twenty-foot expanses on each side of the shop were sturdily framed and fronted with pegboard that displayed an amazing array of clocks that epitomized modern technology and design. I could see keyholes in perhaps three out of approximately 40 on display, the rest of which either had a cord coiled below them or a tiny tag that read, "Battery Operated." Several clocks were fashioned in scrolled wrought iron; others illustrated varying interpretations of star bursts in brass; a couple were crafted in wood; and the remainder were plastic, some of which were labeled "simulated wood" but the majority of which could have been collectively labeled, "The Crayola© Clock Collection."

As we stepped past the wall case, a large archway opened to a room on my left. Setting back from the opening was an institutional-looking blond wood desk with an old Underwood manual typewriter on its surface. Another desk that sat in the corner with a lamp attached would strangely require one to sit at full pos-ture to write at chin level. The ceiling in this room was as proportionately high as the desk. And, due to its 10 by 25-foot dimensions, it seemed more like a hallway than a room. Along the back wall, hidden from the showroom, was a cash register on a small counter and tiers of wrapping paper and ribbon stored on dispensing racks.

"We call this the wrapping room," Mick said as he and Bill brushed shoulders in opposite directions. "That's Molly's desk," he said, pointing at the blond garage-sale wannabe. "We'll teach you how to use the cash register if you haven't done that before," which, of course, I hadn't. "We do free gift wrapping for any purchase," came the sales pitch. There are papers of all colors: paper with little baby buggies, paper with wedding bells, Christmas paper, silver paper, and a roll of white paper plentiful enough to print the *Pershing Daily Journal* for a year. These were all standing by or mounted behind a massive, leather-topped chest.

What really caught my attention in the "wrapping room," however, was a contraption on the matching chest against the opposite wall. "...and this is my baby," Mick continued. It looked part erector set, part Spirograph, part spider—a tinkerer's dream.

"I do the engraving and we do a lot. I'm going to teach you how to use the machine so you can fill in while I'm on vacation."

My prospects were picking up—this looked like play instead of work! And since Sherm walked right past this room without a pause when he came in, maybe he'd leave me alone in here. As I drifted into reverie, the phone jolted me back to reality; it didn't have the gentle purr of the sleek, modern, touch-tone phones at home, but a harsh ring that shook the receiver in its cradle.

"You might as well get started," Mick suggested as he read the hesitation in my eyes. "Just answer: 'Wynn & Scutter' and find out what you can do for the caller."

I hustled to the phone, the same one Mick had used to speak with the alarm company. I watched for Sherm as I headed in his direction, as I knew he was back there—somewhere.

I reached for the receiver but came up short and fell flat on my face. I had seen the phone resting on a shelf behind the showcase in a small alcove at the back archway. What I hadn't seen was the sloped, six-inch incline up to the room behind the arch that tripped me now. Mick laughed hysterically as I scrambled to my feet and grabbed the receiver, which felt like a steel ingot in my hand. "Good morning. Wynn & Scutter Jewelers. May I help you?"

Behind the arch, a counter divided the room nearly in two. I could see Sherm out of the corner of my eye; he was doing the leaning thing again, peering over his eyeglasses at me, his head bowed, his face drawn and stoic. His glasses had a binocular attachment on them.

I listened to the voice on the phone, then placed my hand over the mouth-piece and announced, "I have a customer here who wants to know if his watch is ready."

I didn't dare look at Sherm, who, given half a chance, probably would have whacked me over the head to put me out of his misery. Mick was my only salvation here, even though his attempt to stifle his amusement over my graceful full gainer was pretty feeble.

"What's his name?" Mick sputtered.

"I don't know. He didn't say."

Mick sobered up quickly. I sensed his perception of me was swaying to Sherm's side. "Well then, what's his ticket number?"

"I don't know that either. What's a ticket number?" I asked.

"Heh, heh, heh," Sherm snickered.

"We take their name when they leave a repair and we give them a claim check with a job number," explained Mick. His glance communicated that I was no longer amusing. It was time for business.

"Oh," I responded, like the suave, articulate, sensible fella I was. "Sir, may I have your name and claim check number?" I slapped my hand back over the mouthpiece. "It's Les Johnson but he doesn't have his number."

"I'll take care of it, Mick," Sherm said, and turned around to reach for something.

At that moment I felt secure only because I had the steel ingot receiver in my hand—a potential weapon of defense. Sherm turned back toward me, wristwatch in hand, a white string and ticket hanging from the strap. I was relieved. He analyzed the ticket and the face of the watch for a moment.

"Tell him it's ready," Sherm slowly and deliberately instructed me, the way an adult would teach a child to talk. "Just finished it yesterday and it's right on time. Tell him the charge is $16.50 and he can pick it up any time. Maybe I better talk to him?"

I raised my hand slightly and relayed the information. Sherm lowered his head and peered over his glasses at me again. I finished telling Mr. Johnson his watch was ready, thanked him for calling, and hung up the phone. I looked at Sherm with absolute fear and total admiration. He was a watchmaker.

I have admiration for anyone who can fix things—like my grandfather. He could fix anything, and he had been passing those time-honored talents along to my brothers and me, but he died when I was quite young. We got well through the taking-apart of things, but we never got to the putting-back-together part, which somehow miraculously occurred between our visits.

We should have practiced the skills he tutored us in, but we graduated instead to more important boyhood ventures, like how many rolls of caps we could detonate with the single blow of a hammer, whether the jet engines ordered from bubble gum wrappers really worked, and whether the hovercraft—built from the plans we had ordered—could traverse the rice paddies at Houghton Lake. (By the way, the number of cap rolls was six; the engines pushed a model car for about two feet; and financing the construction of the hovercraft would have required mowing 4,763.6 lawns in one summer.)

"Have a brain fart, did ya?" Sherm asked me as Molly came through a dark doorway to the back room, taking a long drag on a cigarette.

"You leave Steve alone," she chided, waving her smoke around in front of her. "Let him get used to working here before he has to get used to you."

Sherm would not be bested. "You haven't seen the boy walk yet. Don't stand too close or he'll take you down with him."

Molly smiled and ignored him, proceeding to explain my surroundings, guiding me around the room. Sherm's lip-level desk was actually a "bench," and there were two of them against the same wall. "We used to have more watchmakers," she said, "but there aren't many left these days." The second bench was a duplicate of the one in the wrapping room, barren except for the lone lamp on top. Sherm's, however, was piled several inches deep with metal parts and packages, the largest of which was small enough to fit effortlessly through the mouth of a pop bottle. Sherm was hunched over the bench, working in a cleared area roughly the size of a dinner plate.

"You've learned already to stay away from Sherm, I think," observed Molly. "Stay away from the parts on his bench—if you even so much as touch that God-awful mess, he claims he can't find anything." Her cigarette drew all kinds of crazy smoke patterns in the air around me. I wanted to grab her arms to stop their flailing about when Sherm perked up again.

"If you reach for anything on my bench, you'll get a feel of my pigsticker and draw back a bloody stub," came a muffled threat, spoken into the bench.

The counter next to him was designed for storage, with shelves, drawers and open cubbyholes on the back side. The shelves were loaded with tattered old books, manuals, and assorted-sized metal drawer units with labels tucked into slots like the archives at the library.

The large cubby holes near Sherm's bench housed an electronic device that resembled the teletype machines I'd seen in movies, because a small strip of paper streamed out of it, drooping and trailing into a curled pile on the floor. I imagined the machine coming to life, spitting out paper..."ritt-a-da...ditt-a-da...

ditt-a-da," and Sherm leaping to his feet to read off the news: "FLASH! Idiot kid goes to work for prominent business. STOP. Loses job in first 15 minutes. STOP. Couldn't talk, couldn't walk, and couldn't defend self against mean old man with sharp object. STOP."

Molly noticed my interest in the machines and explained that the printing device was a watch-timing machine. Next to that, resting almost at floor level, was another machine that held four clear jars, each containing a different colored fluid and extending on an arm around a central shaft. Sherm lit up a smoke and ignored us. Molly was able to continue without interruption, her cigarette still dancing through the air like a bouncing ball sing-a-long. "…and that thing is a watch cleaning machine." The room started to fill with smoke.

Molly's tour continued as we turned toward the back of the room. "This is Mick's desk," she said as she nodded toward a huge wooden desk that filled the remainder of the space. It was so large, in fact, that there was only room for one person to move around it on any side. The desk was piled with small cardboard boxes, yellow coin envelopes with notes, paper with notes, note cards, note card files, pieces of jewelry, watches and notebooks, all neatly organized and accessible. Above the desk, facing the showroom floor, hung a five-foot-tall clock with a big brass pendulum, rhythmically singing out, "tick…tock…tick…tock," the rhythm occasionally broken with, "buzzzzzzzzzzz, clunk…tick…tock…tick… tock."

The phone clanged again. Mick came flying from the front of the store, I was sure it was to prevent any slight possibility that I might even consider picking it up.

As Molly grabbed a receiver on the big desk, Mick halted amidst a dead run and stood with an enormous look of relief on his face. Molly set her cigarette on the edge of the counter, ashes curved and ready to break off.

"Hi, Maggie…No he's not in yet…Oh, well he should be here any time then…Okay, I'll have him call when he gets in. Good-bye."

Molly's lips never missed a beat. The receiver traveled only about a half-inch back to its cradle when she looked at me and resumed the tour again. "Let's show you the rest so we can get busy. Dale's on his way."

I hadn't noticed the front of the room because I was terrified to take my eyes off Sherm. Molly strutted around the counter, leaving the smoking cigarette butt poised on the edge.

Still relishing his relief over my not answering the phone, Mick looked at the now-smoldering counter. "Molly, I swear! You are going to burn the place down one of these days!" he said, pointing at the fire hazard.

Molly rasped out a chuckle, scurried back around the counter, grabbed the butt, dumped it in Sherm's ashtray, and returned to her starting position in one smooth motion. "There, now get to your own business" she said. Without missing a beat again she pointed at a larger version of a bench built into a cubicle at the front near the arch. Mick turned and left for the wrapping room.

"This is Billy's bench. He's a genius with jewelry. He can do anything as long as you don't rush 'im. He doesn't answer the phone and he doesn't talk to customers. A better goldsmith never lived, so listen to everything he tells you."

Now I was confused. While Bill was geeky looking, he was the most cordial of the group, had presented the most honest smile, and was the least intimidating. But now *he* was the antisocial one.

"Pressure—he hates pressure," Molly continued. "If there's a problem or someone's in a rush, talk to Mick or Dale and they'll figure out how to handle it."

I wondered if anything in the shop was uncomplicated.

The phone clanged. When Sherm answered on an extension at the counter next to his bench I realized there were three phones, all strategically placed within 12 feet of each other. A single phone would require a sprinter or a high jumper to traverse obstacles in the room. Two people intent on answering the same phone without diligently charting and coordinating their trajectories could do some serious head bashing.

Sherm conversed for a moment, hung up, and hollered, "Mick, you gotta get yer butt in gear and open the safes. They're already callin'."

Mick reappeared from the wrapping room, "Don't get all bent outta shape, Sherm," he responded with a defensive smile and high-pitched pleading voice. "I'm on it." He rounded the arch and headed into a hallway off the side of the room.

Molly poked another cigarette between her lips, struck a match, pushed the matchbook in her pocket, plucked the cigarette back out of her mouth, and turned to Sherm. "Maggie said Dale's got a watch he picked up last night. The customer needs an estimate first thing this morning. He's supposed to call as soon as you have it done."

"Can't very well look at something that ain't here, can I?" Sherm commented.

Bill entered from the darkened doorway at the back of the room, his topcoat now replaced by a blue denim work apron. Clip-on blue suspenders held his pants up on his pudgy framework. "Don't even think about pollutin' my space, Molly. You take that thing someplace else, preferably out in the back forty. There's already a haze in here so thick I can't see where I'm goin'," he said, traversing the short distance to his cubicle.

Seeming disgusted in her defeat, Molly whipped the match around in the air until it was just a smoldering version of its former self and sent it, trailing smoke, into a waste basket at Bill's feet. "I'm going to vacuum," she announced, and retreated to the darkness in back.

Bill smiled over his victory. He slathered Corn Husker's Lotion generously over his hands. "This is the place where all the work gets done. Everybody brings their prized possessions to us after they've been someplace else to have 'em fixed."

"Yeah," added Sherm, "they get 'em fixed real good, then bring 'em here for us to repair them!"

Bill laughed as Sherm hunched over his bench.

*　　*　　*　　*

Grabbing a magnifying visor off the shelf, Bill pulled it onto his bristly head and sat down on a leather chair with wheels. He whirled right and left, turning on gas cylinders, flicking switches, and organizing tools. His smile never left his face as we proceeded to get acquainted while he prepared to work. Billy T. Gail reintroduced himself—Billy was his given Southern name. "I was born and raised on a farm in Tennessee, brother of three, son of two, one percent farmer and 99 percent craftsman."

The accidental fact that my father was a medical doctor—coupled with my inclination toward following in his footsteps—seemed to afford me some kind of advanced genetic status in Bill's eyes. I knew that Sherm, quietly hunched ten feet away over his bench, could hear me as I rattled off about myself to Bill. I mentioned my membership in the honor society at school and that I had taken Latin, advanced science, and English classes. As I went on and on, Sherm certainly had little doubt about the quality of our current educational system, most likely conjuring up images of a mailman or milkman to whom I held an uncanny resemblance.

While Bill and I were shootin' the breeze, Mick opened two very large, very old vaults in the hallway across the room. When the door of the second vault thumped open against the wall, he pulled a towel and squeeze bottle from a shelf, carried them over, and thrust them in my hands. "Every day," he said, "the counters have to be cleaned until they shine. Every time a customer or one of us smudges anything, it has to be cleaned."

Molly went zipping by with a smoke flailing in one hand and a rumbling old vacuum following behind her, bumping into every stationary object she passed, including desks, counters, walls, and people.

Prior to my arrival, I had envisioned myself standing behind counters, selling huge diamonds to wealthy executives and young couples in love. Reality, however, was shaping up to resemble boot camp instead of caviar and cocktails. No matter, though. After all, this was only a three-month stint.

I trooped out to the showroom, following Molly with her vacuum   two brave soldiers baring their weapons and headed into battle. She rumbled and bumped all the way up front to the tiny gate, stationed the vacuum in the center of the room, propped her cigarette on the counter's edge, and then tossed the cord back to me. "Plug that in, Hon, will ya?"

I pulled the cord to the nearest outlet. I believe the receptacle was a Thomas Edison demo model, as it was so old and battered the plug barely held in place.

When the phone clanged, Sherm answered. It clanged again, Mick answered, and Sherm kept talking. "Oh, boy," I thought, "two lines!" This could pose a real challenge…

*   *   *   *

The door sounded, "Ding…clank." Uncle Dale, salt and pepper mane on top and finely tailored suit below, stopped halfway over the threshold. He looked at me, grinned, tilted his head, and made his first announcement of the day in a teasing voice: "My top crew is here!"

"Well, whad-a-ya think?" Dale asked as he completed his entrance. "This is a good bunch. They all worked for Jody Wynn for years."

"Good afternoon, Dale," chirped Mick, his head poking around the corner.

"Maggie's waitin' for an estimate," Molly interrupted.

"Hi, Molly. Good *morning,* Mick."

Mick disappeared again. Dale handed a brown paper bag to Molly, which she carried into the back room. Sherm was standing in wait for the hand-off over his counter.

"Hi, Uncle Dale," I chimed in as I weighed my response to his query.

"You ever tell Maggie we go home to sleep at night?" voiced Sherm, loud enough to be heard up front while he rummaged through the bag.

"Mornin', Sherm."

"Hey," the watchmaker uttered as he hunched back over his bench.

Dale turned back to me. "Maggie runs a small shop I lease at the mall in Alaidon. They're open till nine at night, so I stop to exchange repair jobs on my way home. I stop in the morning at South Persy before I come in. I'm going to have you make that run in the morning now that you're here, 'cause 'Smelly Nellie' won't quit talking and I can't get outta there. You find your way here okay?"

"Uh-huh," I said.

"You met Sherm and Bill?"

"Uh-huh," I replied.

"I see they've got you on a project already."

"Uh-huh."

Dale had a strange look on his face, as though I had had a stroke or something. Actually, I was ready to spill the beans and tell him exactly what this kid thought about walking into a den of vile heathen sadists, when Molly scampered back through the gate and flipped the switch on the vacuum. The noise bounced off the walls and rattled the glass in the cases. It sounded like a compactor, the kind that makes a gambling die out of a Studebaker. Our one-sided conversation ended and Dale gave a silent wave and headed for the rear of the shop.

The first squirt from the spray bottle threw me back to catch my breath and wipe the tears from my eyes. The corrosive fumes of ammoniated solution were so strong I didn't know if they wanted the glass cleaned or if the stuff was supposed to melt a fresh gleam into the surfaces. I persisted, however, dousing, scrubbing, and buffing every top, bottom, front and back of every piece of glass, including the windows in the storefront. The entire time I wished I had a clothespin for my nose.

*   *   *   *

Along the way and throughout the days that summer I plucked and disposed of Molly's ashless cigarette butts perched precariously on the edge of every horizontal surface within her reach. Ashtrays were placed strategically around the showroom, but she avoided ever using them. Every combustible surface edge was riddled with evenly spaced, blackened marks, making the oak and maple appear like zebrawood.

For days I eavesdropped on conversations with customers and over the phone. I followed Molly, Mick, and Dale to locate or initiate repairs and to learn about the multitudinous variety of gems and gemstone-metal combinations. Some days I was able to assist, and I slowly learned to recognize when my prying eyes and ears were not welcome, usually sensing this from a customer, or from Mick.

I redeveloped my vocabulary for brief encounters with Sherm. His vocabulary disintegrated rapidly, however, into a series of grunts and one-syllable responses.

Conversations with Molly were primarily gossipy interludes of fascinating tidbits she gathered during her twice-daily coffee clutches with "the girls." As it turns out, Molly is the sister of Jody, one of the founders of the business. A fixture at the shop for 20 years, Molly would have been bored stiff at home with no one to talk to but her husband, who, I am sure, has had little opportunity to squeeze a word in during their 30+-year marriage.

Conversations with Bill were fun, witty, full of old yarns, and usually educational. Bill always explained his work to me, his hands working just as adeptly as his lips during our chats. I learned quickly that getting something done in a hurry by Bill was best accomplished by watching while he worked. Not only was he talented, but he was quite a showman as well. Talks with Mick and Dale were usually brief and utilitarian, and daily talks with the sorrowfully-named "Smelly Nellie" were delightful.

HOW TO GET IN THE
JEWELRY BUSINESS

As the summer wore on, my daily charge—after janitorial duties—included making the trip to South Pershing Jewelry, or "South Persy," as we called it. "Smelly Nellie," as playfully referred to by Uncle Dale, was a dead ringer for Julia Child—same hairstyle, same lips, same posture, and same delightfully amusing voice. The only difference was the laugh. Smelly Nellie could enter a room full of the most desperately depressed souls and leave—in short order—with the whole lot clutching their guts with laughter. She also happened to be Dale's mom. Her jovial nature exuded the rare sort of happiness that rose from the depths of her soul, then reached out and pulled everyone in.

Years later, at a family gathering, Nellie related to me the fate-riddled history of her family's business, told with a great deal of head bobbing, knee slapping, table pounding, and gut hugging. When she met Dale's father, John, she owned and operated a purveyor of delectable delights, aptly named "Nellie's Diner," situated directly across the road from the main entrance of the Pearl Motor Car Company. She worked 16-hour days, six days a week to accommodate her customers, mostly auto workers. "Soup for breakfast, soup for lunch, soup for dinner," she said. "No matter what I cooked, no matter how much time or money I spent preparing anything else, all they ever wanted was my soup. Soup cost a nickel a bowl. I couldn't get ten cents outta those guys for nothin,'" she told me. "Soup, soup, soup. That's all they wanted was soup."

Nellie leaned close to whisper in my ear. "Ya know what?"

"No, what?" I turned my head closer.

"I hate soup!" she whispered, so as not to raise her long-gone soup fanatics from the grave. Then she jolted back in her chair with a thump, her hands dancing in the air, and joyfully cried, "Haven't cooked soup in 30 years!"

John was already a talented, well-established bait-dangling horologist. (In layman's terms that's a watchmaker with a strong penchant for fishing.) His profession garnered loads of respect, but no more compensation than any other depression-era job. Watch owners kept their timepieces in good repair; a good watch was as essential to life and living then as a computer is today, but repair prices corresponded to people's incomes, which were slim to nil at the time, and competition was fierce.

John had dreams of owning a shop of his own, but their holdings were limited to Nellie's Diner; a vacant lot around the corner; a few furnishings in their tiny rented apartment; a beat-up squeaky old Ford, and newborn baby Dale.

Working on a contract basis for jewelers in the greater Pershing area, John took work here and there wherever he found it, like all the other watch repairmen who couldn't make ends meet, and he fished when he couldn't work. The diner continued to provide the basic means for feeding and clothing the expanding family while John's dream lingered. To provide a more steady income, he enlisted in the Air Force, signed up for flight school, and sent his monthly stipend home.

Shipped out to Europe to dominate empires across the ocean, John yearned only to attack the trout-infested lakes of northern Ontario. While he was away, Nellie eked out an existence by working longer hours in the diner across the road from the smoke-spewing factory, which was now re-tooled to build fighter planes instead of motorcars. Business was bleak as more and more women joined the line at the factory, bringing home-packed box lunches, and fewer men visited the diner for the watery soups Nellie miraculously created from rationed goods. Unfortunately, longer hours only translated into fewer bowls.

When John returned safe and unharmed from the still-raging war, he found his earning power decreasing. In those times, most jewelry store owners were watchmakers and goldsmiths in their own right. Because all manufacturing was geared toward the war effort, most businesses—particularly those selling luxury items, such as jewelry stores—found their stock and sales dwindling due to a worldwide shortage of disposable income.

During the war years, diamonds and platinum—the craze of the early 20th century and both primarily obtained overseas—were essential to the manufacturing processes of military equipment. Jewelry stores existed, for the most part, as pawn shops and repair centers. Since the vast majority of gems were mined on other continents, irretrievable due to intervening German and/or Japanese navel fleets, not a single sparkling treasure entered the United States unless it was secreted in by way of Mexico or in the pocket of a homecoming G.I. Store owners worked longer hours, keeping their repair work in-house for the noble purpose of feeding their own families.

John continued to fish when he couldn't work, touring the countryside for fresh lakes and rivers wherever his now rickety, beat-up, even squeakier Ford dared take him. While he deceived the inhabitants of the wild waters, Nellie cleverly deceived the hambone in her stockpot to make ever more transparent soups. At week's end, the two combined their meager earnings to pay for life's necessities. John prepared their staple diet of fried fish, and he dreamed.

*   *   *   *

As the end of the war approached and G.I.s returned stateside, U.S. industry gradually resumed peacetime manufacturing. Lonely war brides were reunited with their long absent husbands and as the economy began to boom, demand for some of life's luxuries began to grow in earnest. John's skills were once again in demand and his income grew steadily, but the capital he needed to realize his dream for the vacant lot around the corner from the diner still seemed beyond his reach.

The war ended abruptly. Everyone came home and the economy boomed. For the first time in 20 years, John found himself turning work away, and Nellie was able to put her old hearty soup recipes back on the diner menu. Their combined income enabled them to live as never before; however, as the economy grew, so did their little boy. "It seemed," recollected Nellie, "that he could eat more than a dozen factory workers could, and the more he ate, the taller he got! It was bad enough to feed him and buy new clothes every month, but we didn't fit in our three-room apartment any more. We spent all we had and then some to buy a house, using up our savings for the store. John quit going to the vacant lot and decided to put it up for sale, but just before he listed the property, the darn factory workers went on strike. Then property and businesses in that part of town wasn't worth nothin.'"

As the economy boomed and everyone else seemed to be getting a piece of the pie, the pies at the diner were going uneaten. Nellie tells the story best.

"Now-a-days the factories only go on strike in the summer. They send a handful of people to walk a picket line while the rest take their union-subsidized wages and go on vacation till it's over. Back then, every worker came and walked the lines 24 hours a day. They carried picket signs, walked, stood, sat, or slept right there. They blocked the gates and the roads. Worst of all for us, they had no money, so they couldn't buy my food at the diner. Once in a while the union representatives bought some food, but they usually brought it in on trucks to feed everybody so they could keep up the strike. We were losin' money like crazy, so I quit cooking very much.

"I kept goin' to work every day to keep the diner open, hopin' the strike—which began in the fall—would end. I felt so bad for those people because the winter was one of the coldest we'd had in years. They stood over fires they built all over the place, but they were freezin'. They didn't come in to the diner much, 'cause they felt bad for me, too. They knew they couldn't buy my food, so they stayed out, and so did everybody else 'cause they were blocking the diner as much as they were blocking the factory.

"One bitter cold day the union men came into the diner. They said the strike was lasting longer than they thought and they needed to feed all the strikers and keep 'em warm. They wanted to know if they could rent the diner—lock, stock and barrel. They didn't want me or the food I had there, but they paid rent and promised that everything would be returned in good condition.

"I didn't know what to do. I couldn't reach John, as he was working God knows where, rent was coming due, I hadn't made but a few dollars in weeks, and one of the men in a suit said he had to have an answer right away. So I packed up all the food, signed a paper the man in the suit had for me, gave 'em the keys, and I left.

"John was mad when he came home that night. Ohhhh, he was soooo mad! He wanted to know why I didn't barter for a few dollars more than the rent, or why I didn't just stay and cook and have them pay me…. why, why, why. He named a million things I should'a done to make some money, but all I wanted to do was get outta there. I didn't even read the paper, just signed it and left.

"Turned out the strike lasted over three more months. John was finally happy I'd turned over the diner because we would have lost a lot. Who would ever know that thing would last so long? I wasn't looking forward to going back. I was having fun being home. I didn't have to cook soup.

The day after the strike was over, the union men called for me to come to the diner. It was dirty, but everything seemed in order. They thanked me for what I'd done for them and set a big stack of papers on a table for me to sign.

The man in the suit explained that rent had been paid directly to the landlord, but I had to sign these papers for them to pay the rent they had promised me. If I hadn't been in such shock, I might'a opened my fat mouth and told 'em the building rent was all I thought they were payin'. They could'a picked up the papers and left and I wouldn't have known any difference.

"The man in the suit flipped through the pages, pointing to lines where I needed to sign. I didn't read nothin'. Like before, I just signed where he told me. While I was writing, they thanked me over and over for letting them use the diner. When I signed the last paper, the man in the suit thanked me again and handed me a check. I looked at it and I almost died—I almost dropped dead right there on the diner floor!"

Although she was literate, Nellie did her "readin' and writin'" in her own, otherworldly way. When stressed or under time constraints, she regressed to a cryptic, phonetic shorthand. A jewelry repair job for a lady's ring, for example, might read, "Hurry 4 good bottom make top 6 good OK." I have seen letters she's written composed of actual complete sentences, compiled into thoughtful paragraphs with proper punctuation. Under pressure, however, Nellie processed paperwork in a way only a handful of souls have ever successfully deciphered. Those garbled instructions should translate as, "Rebuild thinning shank. Size to a 4. Re-tip six prongs. Clean and polish. Customer has consented to appropriate costs. RUSH!"

As a matter of history, Smelly Nellie's naively conceived deal with the man in the suit was not unlike hitting the jackpot in Vegas. The original agreement, which she had neither read nor requested for her own files, reimbursed her for each day's rent at an amount roughly equivalent to what she might earn for three month's hard labor at the diner. In short, Nellie would have had to boil hambones and shovel soup for the rest of her days to amass such a sum!

The diner never reopened. Nellie's windfall enabled the long-struggling couple to erect a building on their vacant lot and inventory a modern jewelry store. With modern equipment and a choice location smack in the center of bustling, booming downtown Pershing, the shop flourished. John realized his dream and Nellie got the wish she had never dared to hope for: she became a full-time stay-at-home mom.

*   *   *   *

The new freedoms provided by a thriving business in the post-war economy allowed John and Nellie to send their handsome, energetic son to college, where he earned his degree in business and then proceeded to the finest horology school in the country. Dale returned home to hoist his shingle under his dad's. He possessed his mother's good humor, business savvy exceeding his father's, and an endearing, gentle nature. These attributes served him well over the years, but were not alone enough to navigate life's fateful crossroads; he also inherited his mother's dumb luck.

Dale and John worked alongside each other for several years. While the arrangement finally gave John the time to attack the Ontario trout that had been goading him for so long, the very independent Dale found himself a mere employee in his father's business.

Seeking a challenge and without his family's knowledge, Dale researched the business climates for an established jewelry store for sale in a growing community. He found exactly what he was looking for in the thriving downtown of the small community of Ithaca. He even began negotiating the purchase of the new business without informing John of his intentions, sure that his dad would be proud. Instead, John was livid. All he could see was the business, Dale's schooling and training, and all the hard work intended to create a legacy with no one to take it over—not the scenario he had envisioned.

Disappointed, John decided to retire, able to do so because the seed money for the business had come as a fortuitous windfall rather than a bank note. Now valuable due to its location, the once-cheap property supported a prosperous business as well. Real estate and old business income alone could keep John and Nellie comfortable for the remainder of their years.

The booming economy, promoting "cars in every garage and chickens in every pot" extended to "a watch on every wrist, a ring on every finger, a clock on every mantle, and china and silver in every cabinet," a great deal of which had been sold at South Persy during the past decade. As Dale took control of South Persy, John retired and took the controls of a brand new floatplane so he could attack the trout with fervor.

*   *   *   *

A busy little store, South Persy fulfilled the dreams of its second-generation owner for several more years, as Dale's endearing demeanor and mechanical skills brought ever more people into the shop. The factory across the street—a proud monument to the vitality of the city—kept forging vehicles from raw steel and sending its workers home with paychecks that were often shared with South Persy.

Of the labors associated with the shop, Dale cherished, above all, his occasional travels to jewelry shows. While examining cases and rolls of merchandise presented by manufacturers' representatives in his shop, Dale listened to and envied their stories about touring the country to show their wares. While they thought it tedious and boring, Dale thought it exciting and adventurous, so he attended jewelry shows whenever he could, flying to New York or other venues at every opportunity. He took seminars, bought merchandise, and mingled. Dale was a good mingler—comfortable discussing merchandise, trends, equipment, and technique with anyone—and he mingled every chance he got. His love of travel remained limited to jewelry shows until fate visited South Persy.

*   *   *   *

A conglomerate of businessmen in the jewelry trade unified to lead the industry into the future. They had developed the concept of a national chain of jewelry stores, all bearing the same name and offering similar merchandise. The new EuroWatch Shop Corporation began to sweep the eastern half of the United States, buying out small, established Mom and Pop operations by offering unprecedented retirement plans to the owners. The concept required instant exposure in choice locations, with no time to build new facilities. South Persy was a perfect target.

The conglomerate's retirement plans offered fixed, long-term payments rather than cash buyouts. With terms set and owners removed, EuroWatch management was poised to take over with its own corporate employees. Financial wizardry and substantial monetary backing allowed the corporation to build a solid infrastructure by buying out prime business locations. The final step in the plan required finding an experienced, youthful, educated individual with local business savvy to monitor inventory, examine trends and procure merchandise for the stores. This was honey in the pot for Dale.

The deal for South Persy differed from others in that in addition to the "retirement plan," Dale was offered the buyer's position and an enormous salary. Even John felt the pot so sweet that only a fool could turn it down. The package included travel expenses for frequent visits to most states on the east coast, in the Midwest and as far south as the Caribbean. Dale packed up and stored his horology tools, then packed his suitcase and became a jet-setter with a weekend home on an island in the Bahamas. Life was good.

The arrangement lasted two years. When a "retirement" payment was 60 days past due, Dale flew to New York to meet with the officer of the company who had originally recommended him for the buying position. Dale learned that the company had overextended by growing too quickly and that there was no recourse other than filing for bankruptcy, which would occur within weeks. All of the retired business owners would have to repossess their stores at some financial loss.

Putting his business savvy to work, Dale demanded possession of assets to off-set his losses before the bankruptcy occurred. Caught off guard by his direct and determined nature, the company assigned ownership of South Persy back to Dale. The only tangible assets the company held beside the scores of businesses that reverted to their original proprietors was a seasonal shipment of fine Swiss watches previously held up in U.S. Customs and currently stored at a New York warehouse. Thanks to his business acumen, Dale not only became the owner and operator of South Persy again, he also became the owner of enough watches to inventory a hundred stores just like it.

*   *   *   *

Dale reluctantly settled back into the small town lifestyle he had shunned for martini lunches and Bahamian weekends. He hired his own sales representative to travel and sell the thousands of wristwatches, and together they were able to liquidate the entire inventory within a year. Thanks to his ability to capitalize on the inside information from the conglomerate, Dale was now content, wiser, and richer, and his hired rep was happy with his generous commission.

*   *   *   *

The demise of the EuroWatch Company was a result, in part, of sweeping societal change and cultural evolution that affected traditional retailers. Suburban sprawl replaced urban stability and shopping malls sprang into existence on the outskirts of every major city in the country. The malls were always built on some-one's granddaddy's papa's farm outside traditional social and economic centers. The Big Bang theory of urban decay had begun. Families fled for miles in every direction, leaving a cloud of settling city dust at the core.

Dale held two beliefs: that the strengths and traditions of a full-service family jewelry store could outlive the cash-and-carry supermarket-type retailer at the outlying, sterile shopping centers, and that simply outliving the competition wasn't enough. So he leased a small, high-exposure cubicle at a mall in the upscale community of Alaidon. After inventorying with less expensive, impulse-purchase jewelry and watches, Dale displayed large signs to advertise the services he offered, which would compete heavily against the cash-and-carry chain store. Clearly, EuroWatch had been about three years too early, their concept only slightly off target.

Dale hired Maggie to manage Alaidon Jewelry and Watch Repair and protect his interests. The wife of a Baptist minister, her ethical nature was commensurate with her position, and Maggie held a work ethic somewhere between Benjamin Franklin and Attila the Hun. The good fortune of hiring Maggie at the mall not only protected Dale's interests, but helped create yet another profitable venture. Like a drill sergeant on amphetamines, Maggie managed her growing team of employees and expanded her repair business so efficiently that Dale was forced to hire a goldsmith and an additional watchmaker at South Persy to accommodate her demands. Nellie even came back to work, while her son spent his days at the bench. The secret to South Persy's success was the winning combination of Dale at the helm and Nellie at the counter. A loyal following kept the store alive while the city of Pershing deteriorated all around it.

Spoiled by decades of successful independent businesses taking care of themselves and supporting the infrastructure, Pershing municipal government played a duet with Nero's ghost, bleeding the economy for self-serving tax dollars, standing mute while the city crumbled.

A combination of Japanese imports and an uncaring government led to the rapid fall and failure of the Pearl Motorcar Company. Pershing eventually inherited ten city blocks of derelict buildings and environmentally contaminated soil. Businesses in the area—from shoe stores to banks—locked their doors and moved away. Homes that were once proud middle-class dwellings stood boarded up or became cheap rentals. Within a few years the once affluent and influential corridor became a microcosm of the resulting effects of community neglect.

Ironically, the jewelry store continued to profit. A constant influx of repair work from the domineering Maggie and a customer base from the ever-endearing owner ensured stability—at least for a while. Dale knew South Persy's days were numbered, so he began once again to seek a fresh location. This time, however, the new business had to be in his own back yard to carry out the local legacy.

Amazingly, 18 jewelry stores flourished in downtown Pershing, ranging from modern chain stores to traditional Mom-and-Pop operations, all selling similar merchandise, but each with its own niche in the market. Brogan's, Daniel's, Pinker's, Lyman's, Wynn & Scutter, the Gem Market—12 more, plus the department stores managed to fill the needs of local shoppers. But for 40 years, The Gem Market had existed at the bottom of the food chain.

Tattered paths in the threadbare carpet led from the Gem Market's dusty, moisture-stained window displays through the musty showroom to the counter where most business was transacted. The Gem Market no longer sold timepieces or provided services since it had found a niche selling outdated, mismatched, and often substandard jewelry that attracted a steady stream of a particular "sort" of clientele. The place was an eyesore, but it was available and affordable, and it was centrally located in Pershing's downtown business district.

Purchase negotiations transpired quickly, Dale made a substantial down payment, and the store was to be his within one month. With her roots firmly planted in the family business, Nellie opposed the purchase because she felt South Persy, under any conditions, provided a preferable foundation to the Gem Market. John was confident in the knowledge that his son had made good decisions in the past and accepted that Dale would likely do whatever he chose to do. Dale harbored his own reservations about the purchase, but he knew that location was the key to success or failure in the marketplace, so he forged ahead with his plans.

Dale spent sleepless nights and tedious days developing a strategy to reinvent the Gem Market. Inventory had to be closed out and eliminated. Fixtures and amenities needed to be replaced and upgraded, and the landlord had to make significant structural improvements.

Except for location and display cases, every aspect of the store had to be entirely rebuilt, including its reputation.

On the eve of the final transaction, Dale would not rest, haunted by his intuitive businessman's hunch that for once, he had really leapt too fast. Every aspect of the Gem Market tallied up on the wrong side of his pro and con list, and even though Dale had absolute confidence in his abilities, he knew that people's memories were long-lived and their shopping habits too ingrained for the Gem Market to turn around its image in a reasonable time. Dale lay in bed until six o'clock in the morning when he decided to phone the seller and call off the deal. Relieved, Dale forfeited his deposit, considering it a small price for his mistake.

*   *   *   *

Back in South Persy, business returned to normal. Dale buried himself back at his bench beside Ron, his assistant horologist, and Walter, his Russian goldsmith. Nellie joked, laughed, and visited with customers who rarely left without dropping some of their hard-earned cash into her welcoming hands. She giggled and hooted over the cash register as she recounted the tales of her salesmanship, as if they hadn't heard it all while it happened.

South Persy and Alaidon surpassed expectations at every turn. In both shops, the nine-to-five routine ticked away with the precision of the instruments serviced and the loyal employees found themselves firmly ensconced in the ritual machinations of the American dream. Nellie and Dale's dream, however, was abruptly shattered by the news delivered by a police officer on a pleasant, sunny, summer afternoon: John had perished in his plane. The wreckage had been spotted the previous day by a fire survey plane inspecting the remote backwoods of Ontario. It took another 24 hours for Provincial Police to locate the site on foot and identify the pilot.

It was not at all unusual for John to disappear for several days at a time in the summer months while he frequently moored his plane on isolated lakes to fish and camp. In his zealous quest to find bigger, wilder trout, this time he had landed on a lake too small for the doggy flying boat's safe lift-off, imperiled and ultimately prevented by the bowl of virgin pines around the lake.

John had faced obstacles and overcome the odds all his life. This time the stakes were too high and the odds too heavy. Nellie's laugh was dampened for some time. Dale learned the truth of carrying on a legacy—the gift is often packaged in sadness. John's independent life had been touched throughout by twists of fate. In the end, fate was not on his side.

✳   ✳   ✳   ✳

During the spring of 1974, Dale inspected the trays of rings laid out on his counter by a sales representative from Chicago. While he admired and selected pieces for his store, they engaged in the gossipy banter that always accompanied a buying session. As the conversation eventually led to Pershing's current business climate, the rep mentioned that at his largest account in town, Wynn & Scutter, he hadn't made a single sale because Jody Wynn planned to find a buyer and retire at the end of the year. Abruptly ending the sales meeting, Dale phoned Jody, arranged to meet downtown at Walgreen's Drug Store for coffee, and was out the door within ten minutes.

Jody confirmed the rumor and within one hour of hearing the news, Dale agreed to the price and terms Jody proposed, sealing the deal with a handshake and a smile. It was agreed that Dale would take possession of his new business the following January 2, before which they would work together for several months so Dale could become accustomed to working with his new staff and his clientele could get acquainted with him. Dale initiated the transition in August, dividing his time between South Persy and Wynn & Scutter.

Two months later, on October 1, Jody informed Dale that too many Christmases in retail had taken their toll on him and that he wanted out immediately so he could enjoy a "normal" Christmas for the first time. Jody left at the end of the day and Dale took over the business immediately.

Because Jody honored the original purchase agreement, Dale invested nothing but his time during the following three months. Between his existing businesses and inventory and Jody's business and inventory, enough profit was generated to double his down payment in January.

*   *   *   *

Dale's acquisition, which eventually became his primary business, enjoyed a fine, reputable history. Established more than three-quarters of a century earlier as a family business and developed on a foundation of trust and quality, the store became a major player in the local market under the reins of Jody Wynn and Larry Scutter. The senior Scutter retired in 1955 at age 58 and sold out to Jody Wynn. Jody capably continued his 44 years in the business, with well-deserved admiration and respect from his clients and the community. He walked in the door in financially uncertain times at the age of 18 and stayed until he walked out at age 64. The only time he spent away from the business, except for brief summer and winter vacations, was during his tour of service in World War II.

Once considered lavish in size, the shop's stature was now dwarfed by that of the newer chain stores in the suburbs. Nonetheless, Wynn & Scutter remained firmly rooted in the community, thanks to the people behind the counters who now faced the challenge of accepting into their midst a new boss and ever so briefly, his floundering teenage nephew.

LEARNING FROM THE MASTER

I quickly got into the habit of arriving for work 15 minutes early. Mick always arrived first. I learned fast, as he probably had early on, that anyone other than Dale who arrived after Sherm would receive a verbal beating for tardiness. Anyway, being early allowed for an expedient retreat into the wrapping room, where I could cower and make myself look busy until Sherm planted himself at his bench. My plan wasn't foolproof, however. While there was clearly a Sherm barrier at the archway—his feet never crossed the line into the wrapping room—his head and one shoulder cranked around the corner frequently.

"Yup," he would grumble to my "Good morning" or "Think so?" or "Here again?"

The longest greeting he offered was, "Yeah, yeah, yeah."

Once the phones started ringing and customers began popping in and out, Sherm became approachable, abrupt but responsive, and studiously efficient at his trade. I was constantly amazed at his ability to instantaneously pluck any needed watch part from the gnarled mass on his bench with the agile flick of his tweezers. With equal speed he installed the part and made the timepiece functional again. Tools clicked on his bench like on a surgeon's tray.

Every workstation was engulfed in its own rhythmic melody of function. The constant drone of typewriter keys thrashed their way through a dense, smoky haze and crashed against paper and carbon that surrounded Molly's desk. "Zip, zip, Ziiinggg!" the reel and carriage rang out at intervals and then, "splot!" the paper landed on the pile next to a smoldering cigarette butt. Molly hammered out legible recreations of the short-handed scribbles that came from Dale's appraisal bench.

Dale had forsaken his horology tasks for the art of appraisal, which had been a significant source of income for Jody and a sought-after service to the customers. The larger trade at this store required full-time attention to the duty, so Dale—the only qualified appraiser—filled the position. The sounds emanating from his bench were the "plop" of the hollow, cup-shaped eye loupe every time it was set down, the scratching of pencil on paper, the grinding of the pencil sharpener, the "ping" of gold and platinum in the metal tray of the balance, and the rattle of the micrometer as it is was raised to measure an object and then placed gently back on the glass-topped wood bench. His melody was more monotonous than the others with its "plop, scratch-scratch, ping, scratch-scratch, grind, scratch-scratch, rattle, scratch-scratch, plop."

The repertoire at Bill's bench was the most controversial, with fine-toothed saws and files gently purring as they rhythmically passed through the soft precious metals. The soothing "woosh" of the torch flame dancing gently around the metal, slowly swayed back and forth, softly caressing the shiny creations until they glowed like the vermilion orb at sunset. Finally, as the flame's target reached a physical state between modern artistry and primordial ooze, the metal flowed, moving as if alive. A barely audible "snap" of the torch flame signaled that Bill had closed the fuel supply, followed by a short silence while the object rested. A peaceful "hisssss" sounded when it had rested enough to set in a bowl of water, and a long pause lulled the audience into contentment while Bill examined his fabrication. So in tune with his audience, now thoroughly relaxed and nearly catatonic, "crang"—the sound of steel forging a forgiving cousin resonates when his hammer—wielded from shoulder height, slammed down onto the steel mandrel. Pencil leads crunched into Dale's paper and snapped off. A half-dozen or so keys became entangled and were strewn with ashes in Molly's typewriter, and Sherm jolted into a rare moment of correct posture, cussing under his breath.

Molly mumbled silently while dragging on a cigarette to calm her nerves. Her normally flawless typing was now marred where the garble on the appraisal and carbon copy had to be erased. Dale's pencil sharpener ground away, and Sherm dropped on all fours.

"Pallet fork come your way, Bill?" Sherm asked the silently giggling Bill while he crawled around on the floor.

"Haven't seen it," he responded. "Losin' track of yer parts again, Sherm?"

"Just doing some stretching," he conceded. "Someday, somebody's gonna take that hammer of yours and stretch it across yer…"

"Sherm?" Dale interceded, "you got the Forbes' watch done yet?"

"It's running a bit too smooth, so I thought I'd let the fork gather a little dust and sand down here before I put it back," he responded.

"Bill," Dale continued, "Mrs. Belen has called three times about her ring. Think you can get it finished up soon?"

"I keep all my jobs up here where I can finish 'em. That was done a half-hour ago; you can call her. She'll probably run over three pedestrians to get here."

Whoever coined the phrase "40 years a watchmaker, ten years at the bench, 30 years on the floor" knew exactly what they were saying. Strong knees, a broom, and a dustpan were as important to a watchmaker as his tweezers and screwdrivers as tiny metal parts clamped between the teeth of needle-sharp tweezers frequently took flight like tiddly winks on unknown trajectories. Good ears were as important as good eyes, and Sherm could hear a gnat land on a tissue. Occasionally I would see him freeze in mid-motion to listen for an inaudible "tick" to mark the general direction of his search for a minuscule part. A set bridge—the tiny spring required to hold the stem in a watch—once adorned Molly's permanent wave for two and a half days before a straight-faced Sherm sneaked up behind her and flicked it off with his tweezers, stoically pleased to discover its location.

As the shenanigans continued at the benches, I concentrated intently on my engraving duties. The work itself reminded me of a graphic arts class in junior high school, except that it didn't involve smearing permanent blue ink all over yourself. It did, however, involve the same tedious monotony, and I learned to dislike it in short order. Unfortunately, I was learning to master the blasted skill.

What I really wanted to learn was every word in Mick's vocabulary, every subtle body motion, every nuance of his personality. I was even ready to glue a fake Fu-Man-Chu under my nose. I don't know exactly how many phone calls came every day or how many people walked through the door, but of the 60 or 70 combined, about half were for Mick, and they were all about girls. If it wasn't a beautiful young woman, going about 20 miles out of her way, stopping in to say hello, she was calling on the phone. Or it was one of a small clique of guys calling to talk about a woman who would eventually stop or call. It wasn't five or six woman, or eight or ten; it was dozens and more! I could pick them out instantly when they came in the door, because they responded to my greeting, while their eyes searched stealthily for any indication of Mick. When a girl's senses zeroed in on him, I was routinely brushed off with a frank don't-bother-me-boy-I'm-busy,

Sherm-like attitude. The faces and voices changed constantly; either they got bored with him or he with them—I never knew for sure, but there seemed to be an endless supply. Whatever it was he had, I wanted it.

I wanted so badly to learn the conversational techniques that lured such beautiful women, but whenever I tried to eavesdrop on Mick's phone calls, his magical words became coy how-de-do's. I did learn two indelible facts, however: when a woman of particular interest phoned, Mick would lean his chair back and perch his feet on his desk for a lengthy conversation; and a cocktail lounge across town called the Tiki Hut served a mystical potion, a "Volcano," which must have been formulated by Aphrodite. Apparently every time Mick shared a Volcano with a female, she stalked him for days, with the voracity of a hormone-charged rabbit in heat.

✳   ✳   ✳   ✳

A few years later, when I finally reached the age to legally frequent bars and pubs, I decided to have a go at this fervently potent formula myself. The trick, I figured, was just to maneuver the woman of my dreams to the Tiki Hut, and all the run-of-the-mill tactical wining, dining, and gift buying could be dispensed with; one sip at a Volcano and she would be clawing at my heels for eternity.

My opportunity arose when Brian, a close buddy of mine, told me his cousin had just broken up with her fiancé. I had frequently mentioned how attractive I found her, how friendly she was when our paths crossed, and how I wished she were single.

"Oh, she'll go out with you in a second," Brian said, after hearing of the break-up. "She thinks you're cute."

Somehow I didn't believe Mick's women thought he was "cute," but I had to start the ball rolling somewhere, so I got her phone number from Brian and phoned.

"Hi, is this Janet?" I asked, exuding confidence—one of Mick's special touches.

"Yes, this is Janet."

"Hi, this is Steve, Brian's friend."

"Oh yeah, the cute one. Hi, Steve."

This wasn't right. I had *never* heard any woman say anything remotely like this to Mick—they just drooled, but I guess that was after the Volcano. Maybe it was just early.

"I—I was wondering if you might be free Saturday night. I'm going to get a bite to eat, stop for a drink at a new place I've heard about, then I thought I'd go to the Gables for dancing. They've got a live band there this weekend. Would you care to join me?"

"Sounds fun. What time should I be ready?"

We agreed on a time and I got directions to her parents' house, where she still lived while going to college. Four days passed while I rehearsed phrases and gestures acquired through astute observation of Mick. On Saturday I pulled into Janet's driveway at 7 o'clock, not a minute earlier or later than the agreed-upon time. Of course I hadn't accompanied Mick on a date, so I didn't know if promptness was cool. In hindsight, I figure he would have been about an hour late.

"Hi, Janet," I smiled, looking at her through the screen door.

"Steve, hi. It's nice to see you. I've been looking forward to tonight since you called."

Things were looking up. She had been anticipating our date and she was more beautiful than I remembered. She had huge, green eyes, surrounded by a halo of shiny brown hair, full voluptuous lips that would cause a lipstick model to cringe with envy, and a figure as magnificent as any that had ever graced a woman. She wore a tight knit sleeveless top and a pair of slacks that accentuated every curve of her extraordinary frame. This was a woman who would never have to resort to Volcanoes—her mere presence was dizzying.

The screen door swung open and Janet stepped down onto the porch stoop. My heart sank when I realized that my direct gaze leveled off at the tip of her nose. Far from "tall, dark, and handsome," I was blonde, five-foot-seven, and apparently "cute." Her platform shoes with heavy high heels afforded her at least an inch-and-a-half clearance over my tousled locks.

"Oh, it's chilly out here. I'm going to grab a wrap and I'll be right back," said Janet as she disappeared back through the screen door. Her brief absence allowed me to contemplate the fact that I should have sneaked up behind her with a yardstick before I asked her out. She reappeared with a paper-thin shawl tossed over her shoulders and a pair of ballet slipper-type things on her feet.

"Okay," she said, rearranging the shawl around her shoulders and never mentioning the shoes. "This will keep me comfortable. I'm ready now."

We climbed into my bachelor-mobile—a red, 1970 Chevy Nova that weighed about 50 percent more than its original manufactured poundage—now a rolling advertisement for Bondo and Fiberglass. I had to avoid potholes and railroad tracks for reasons other than the need for new shock absorbers and leaf springs.

The body had been meticulously recreated, and a good thump would cause great chunks of it to fly to the ground and crumble into dust. We meandered our way to my favorite Italian restaurant on meticulously charted, smooth roads.

"I thought we were going to Spazo's!" Janet hollered above the unusually loud music I played on the radio to drown out the car's squeaks and rattles.

"We are!" I shouted back.

"Well, if you had turned back there it would only take about five minutes!" she offered.

People in other cars were staring at us, probably thinking we were having a lovers' spat, the way we were hollering.

"Yeah, but I was afraid we might be held up by a train, and this is a more scenic route," I lied above the din of the Bee Gees.

By now Janet had a terribly confused look on her face. "Are you sure you remember where it is? That way has a golf course and a ballpark. This road will take us by a factory and a construction site!"

"I know!" I yelled back at her. "I like to see the progress they're making clearing the old farm and woods!" It was only a small stretch of the truth, because when I was five years old I wanted to grow up to be "a tractor jockey."

When we finally turned toward the restaurant, Janet's anxieties seemed to fade. We arrived in time for the 7:30 reservation I had made and we both chuckled when we realized our voices were a bit boisterous, our ears still ringing from the loud, roundabout drive. We talked about Brian's antics at her family gatherings when they were growing up and compared notes on college courses. I favored science and literature; Janet preferred math and psychology. After we enjoyed our meal, I suggested we venture onward.

"How 'bout hittin' the road so we can stop for a cocktail before the band starts at the Gables?" I was feeling much more confident now.

"Sure," she said. "Dinner was wonderful. Where we goin'?"

"I've heard of a place I've always wanted to try. It's called the Tiki Hut and it's right on our way."

"No offense," she jeered, "but if we go back the way we came, everything is on the way. It's okay, though. Just could we turn the radio down a little?"

Red-faced but contented, I drove east, then south, then west, and north and east again until we had squeaked and rattled in a zigzag pattern across the entire town, avoiding every change in elevation that exceeded a quarter-inch. Janet was correct; a short diversion from one of the multitudinous neighborhoods we traversed would have landed us at just about any establishment in town. Call it poor planning on my part, but it was my hunch that she would prefer her car door should remain intact for the duration of the date.

We arrived at the Tiki Hut in style. I squeaked, literally, into a parking place among throngs of shoppers returning to their cars from stores in the adjacent shopping center. The bachelor-mobile decided to do its sputtering run-on thing after I turned it off and removed the key. When we were both out of the car, it wheezed its last breath and backfired. As everyone in the lot looked in our direction to see who got shot, I felt like a person who had passed gas in a crowded elevator. Undaunted, Janet laughed and took my arm, aiming us toward the Polynesian style decor on the facade of our destination.

Except for palm fronds over the bar and a few tiki carvings on the walls, the interior of the place betrayed its name. The speakers around the room blared 100 percent American top-20 tunes, and pinball machines whirred and buzzed against the walls. Near the bar, two pool tables consumed a good portion of the room, and a gang of about 15 crowded around a game of skeeball. We found a quieter room in back with cozy, semicircular booths snuggled up against mural-covered walls on which exotic, bubbling fish swam by bare-breasted native women performing daily housekeeping tasks on mountainous tropical islands. We found a comfortable booth in the corner beneath a depiction of a topless young girl weaving baskets, and we sat down.

We had barely wriggled into our seats when a waitress appeared, pad and pencil at ready and impatiently asked, "What can I get ya, guys?"

The moment of truth had arrived. "May I order for us?" I asked Janet, trying to hide the gleam in my eye.

"Absolutely," she said, "I'm in your able hands."

It was all I could do to keep myself from bounding onto the table to scream triumphant hallelujahs.

"We'll have two Volcanoes, please," I ordered suavely.

"I don't think so, Hun," the waitress coldly responded, scrunching her eyes and shaking her head.

Dumbfounded, I sat speechless and devastated.

"Have you ever had a Volcano?" she inquired.

"Well, no. But I heard they are good."

"They are," she replied, "but one Volcano is enough for six people. I could get in trouble if I brought you each one. You guys driving?"

"Yeah, I am."

"Maybe you two better show me some I.D.," she demanded.

In the mid to late 70s, places like this only carded customers they considered prepubescent pretenders at risk of losing their faculties with one drink.

To my chagrin, we produced our identification. While neither of us was a seasoned drinker, we were both old enough to have tipped a few.

"All right, you love birds, what'll it be?" the waitress glared at me through the corners of her narrowed eyes.

At that, every ounce of blood in my body flowed to my face. I could feel my ears burning and my eyes bulging, displaying the wisdom and clarity of thought to which fools such as myself were oblivious.

"Could we share a Volcano?" Janet inquired.

"Yeah, I s'pose, Darlin,'" smirked our server. "One Volcano and two straws, comin' up!"

My date carried the conversation for a few minutes while the blood in my face flowed back to my limbs and vital organs. I made a mental note to do in-depth reconnaissance missions on any future dating destinations to avoid such embarrassment. Janet handled the situation beautifully, though, unknowingly setting the very trap that would make my heart hers forever.

We watched wide-eyed as our waitress returned, bearing the tropical delicacy I had only dreamed about, grandly presented in a huge porcelain facsimile of a natural wonder, surrounded by a moat of syrupy red liquid and topped with flickering blue flames.

"There you are, one Volcano as ordered. Be careful of the rum in the center; it's a killer. That'll be $11.50, young fella."

Eleven-fifty! Dear God—11 dollars and 50 cents! A typical drink cost about 75 cents back then—a buck if it was good stuff. After filling the tank of the bachelor-mobile for the cross-country excursion and paying for dinner, I only had $15 left, not enough to pay this tab and go the Gables, too. I opened my wallet under the table so no one could see the contents, and peeled out $13.

"Keep the change," I said, hoping that after a sip or two of the Volcano Janet wouldn't care about dancing anymore.

The server left us and we stared and laughed at the monstrosity on the table. The outer rim of the bowl was carved with exotic orchids and monkeys hanging from lush vines. The volcano was an erupting goliath, spewing lava the color of the liquid in the moat, which bobbed with ice cubes. The best thing, I thought, would be to dive right in and prove my manhood. I grabbed one of the two-foot-long straws and thrust it into the flaming peak.

"Here goes!" I announced.

"I…" Janet tried to intercede as I sucked in a manly swallow of the fiery brew.

The tip of the straw drooped and the shaft shriveled into the flame as the liquid approached my mouth, blue flames and all. My eyes bolted open in terror as the searing torch searched for my lips.

"...think you're supposed to blow out the flames first," she finished about a half-second too late.

The roof of my mouth, my tongue, and particularly my lips felt as though I had slurped from a vat of boiling oil. I slapped my hands over my mouth to stifle my screams of pain. The look in Janet's face was a perfect combination of shock and hysterical delight.

"Oh my God!" she exclaimed as she fished for ice cubes in the moat and thrust them toward me. "Does it hurt? Put the ice on it, quick!"

I welcomed the cubes in my cupped hands and cradled them against my lips. Red syrupy liquid melted and drizzled down my chin, dripping on my shirt and pants.

"Are you all right?"

"Yef," I answered through the ice. "I fink I'm okay," I lied. I wasn't okay. It hurt like Hell's fury! But I had taken hold of my senses and decided not to scream. Besides, the ice helped numb the pain slightly.

Our waitress returned. "Swift move, Hun. Most amazing thing I've seen all day," she said as she blew out the flames and picked the burning straw from the Volcano with her wet towel and set a replacement on the table. "I suggest you try it without the fire. Here, you look like you need this." She handed me a cool, damp towel and left.

"That *was* amazing!" Janet observed. "Do you know your lips were actually on fire?"

To this day, Janet's observation is emblazoned in my consciousness as the most complimentary thing a woman has ever said to me.

I daubed as much of the drink off my shirt and pants as I could while we laughed at my profound stupidity. At least I had provided the fodder for lively discussion. My hopes for a special evening soared once again as Janet and I propped our straws in the bowl, tasting the magic potion in unison. I gulped more than my fair share of the alcohol, hoping to relieve some of the pain.

The moat contained an overly sweet blend of fruit juices heavily laced with rum. The once flaming peak held an ample supply of high-proof rum, minus the flavoring or dilution. We laughed and drank. The effects were wonderful and I began to feel giddy.

"Your lip."

"I veg your fardon?"

"Your lip. Your upper lip…" Janet said, closely inspecting my face. "Wait." She rummaged through her purse and held out a mirrored compact. "Look at your lip; it's getting all swollen."

I thought the Volcano had started doing its job because Janet had been scooting closer to me as we drank. Now I realized she was just positioning herself for a better view of the grotesque physical transformation of my mouth. My image reflected a hideous, dime-sized blister protruding from a swollen upper lip.

"What?" I casually replied, now in total acceptance of the situation. "You never dated Quasimodo before?"

"I think we'd better go," Janet suggested. "That looks like it hurts bad and it'll probably get worse. You need to get home and put more ice on it."

I agreed that our plan to go dancing was now pretty much out of the question. A swollen lip and two bucks in my pocket wouldn't go far, and now, after wriggling out of the booth into the light, I could see that my Volcano splotched shirt and pants created more of a spectacle than my newly redesigned face. I did, indeed, look rather like a prepubescent pretender who had lost his faculties after just one drink.

As we walked through the flashing lights in the game area, I saw Mick standing at the bar, one foot on the rail, a drink in hand, and three gorgeous women—droopy eyed and drooling—surrounding him. I turned my head away as we shuffled out the door, hoping he wouldn't see me, ever thankful of his undivided attention to females.

I drove a straight line back to Janet's home, inflicting less damage on the Nova than I had on my person. Depositing my date on her doorstep, I presented her with my home and work numbers, still confident that the Volcano would kick in and upon my return home I'd be chatting, feet perched and smiling contentedly, on the phone. Janet gave me a gentle kiss on the cheek and thanked me for an exciting evening.

She never called. A few weeks later when Brian and I got together I inquired about Janet.

"I don't know what you did, but she told me she had more fun with you than she'd had in a long time."

"Really?" I was shocked. "Did she tell you about our date?"

"No, but I suppose I should beat you up or somethin'.'"

"How come?"

"Well, I set you up on a date with my favorite, sweet, fragile cousin, then all I hear about it is that you've got the hottest lips in town."

"Oh, yeah, right! Geez, I gave her my phone number and she never called!"

"That's the depressing part," Brian pointed out while curling his cheeks. "I never could stand the guy, but for some reason she got back together with her fiancé a day or two after your date."

"That's depressing," I reflected.

"Yeah, her sister says they hang out all the time now at some place called the Tiki Hut."

"Tough luck," I thought out loud.

*   *   *   *

At my tender age I had some of the moves, but apparently none of the expert's manner. Mick likely would be proud of my attempt to emulate him, but not impressed with my fledgling results; he didn't deliver women back into their ex's arms. Reflecting back on my days as a youthful victim of wanton desire, I'll always secretly wonder if it was Jimmy Carter's sheer strength of character that enabled him to confine his lust to his heart, or if he, too, took a sip from a flaming Volcano…

MAKING FRIENDS

Seasons arrive of their own accord in Michigan, paying little attention to the cyclical notations on calendars. Jody Wynn claims we have two here: winter and July 6th. The truth is not far off. Spring, a beautiful and hopeful season, lingers well into the scientific definition of summer. One evening you sit in your favorite chair, wrapped in blankets and thermal underwear, shivering in the damp air laden with bird songs and the aroma of fruit blossoms drifting in your open windows. The next morning you awaken to sweltering heat and torrid humidity, setting up every electrical device available to create an artificial breeze.

The climate changes cause the entire population of our state to migrate en mass from the lower one-third to the upper half of its borders. We call it "vacation"; in reality, it is salvation. Nationally, some 80 percent of the population lives near coastal waterways. In Michigan, about 10 percent live near the water, but 99.9 percent vacation there. The remaining 0.01 percent stay home and work—that would include Sherm, myself, and Bill, who was quite content in the heat.

The vacation schedules at the store were staggered to avoid undue workload stress. Molly was pretty much on vacation all the time, popping in and out for coffee clutches, hair appointments, personal emergencies, and general I-don't-wanna-be-theres. A fixture in the store due to her longevity, her strong customer base, and the Wynn family ties made Molly's eccentricities acceptable.

My primary concern was how I would fare in Mick's absence. It was Monday morning. Mick had left after work on Saturday for a two-week vacation. In his absence, my attempts to arrive at work early to avoid Sherm were totally hopeless.

I still had to be there early enough to avoid ridicule, so I held my ground and stuck to the same schedule.

After pacing up and down the sidewalk in front of the store a few times, I leaned against the building and tucked my hands into my pockets to calm myself and forestall hyperventilation. It was comforting to greet a few familiar faces I had gotten to know from nearby stores and offices. Clay's Department Store was bustling with eager employees as usual, and the beauty shop adjacent to us was busier than I expected at this early hour. I kept a sharp eye out for Sherm. He could come from anywhere and I was going to be prepared when he did. I wasn't about to have him sneak up behind me.

People flowed by in both directions; janitors, bankers, store clerks, clerical workers, suits, dresses, and uniforms bounced energetically to whatever the day offered.

The City Pub filled the remaining space between the beauty shop and the cor-ner. An occasional pedestrian dropped from the teeming ranks and peered guiltily in both directions before slipping inside, stopping to put a little extra bounce in his step, I presumed. I'd been in there for lunch, but opting for solid food rather than the liquid nourishment everyone else there favored, felt I didn't fit in. I found the pub too dark inside, with no windows and very low wattage lights, but an unworldly 17-year-old couldn't understand that a more revealing environ-ment would result in the loss of most of the bar's regular customers.

I entertained myself by peering at the rosy-cheeked, parched patrons as they rambled into the pub, but my entertainment ceased as a stony-faced figure loomed over the crowd rounding the corner. It wasn't Sherm—too tall, too pale and too stoic, if that was possible. *Must be one of his henchmen*, I thought amus-ingly as the ominous figure floated through the crowd, oblivious to its presence. He approached, thin and incredibly tall, hands burrowed firmly in the pockets of his open trench coat, strands of thin hair sneaking out from beneath a brimmed hat slung low on his forehead. There was no bounce in his step; it was just a steady, level gate. As he passed, his square-jawed face never moved, but his eyes fixed on me and rotated to their very corners until I escaped his peripheral view. The unbroken gaze between us sent shivers up my spine.

"Ate something bad for breakfast again, eh?" guessed Sherm. Surprisingly, I was relieved to hear his voice as he dropped out of the crowd.

"Mornin'. Whadda ya mean?"

"You got that stupid look on your mug again."

"I was just thinking 'bout somethin'."

"Don't use it up, son. There ain't that much to go around."

Oh man, I thought as I winced, *this is going to be a fun two weeks!*

I followed Sherm through the door, and he made the morning call to security and turned on the lights. Bill arrived shortly behind us, and Dale followed uncharacteristically early.

As everyone settled quickly into his duties, I became acutely aware of the fact that just one missing body, it seemed, doubled everyone's work load—everyone's except mine.

Mick had caught up on all the engraving before he left, so I had little to do. I polished the cases, vacuumed the floors, and answered the phone—a lot.

"Hello, Wynn & Scutter Jewelers. How may I help you?"

"Hello, may I speak with Mick, please?" I can't begin to count the number of times I would hear these same words from so many young ladies' lips during the next two weeks.

"No I'm sorry but Mick isn't in right now. May I take a message?"

"No, thank you. Do you expect him in today?"

"No, I'm afraid he won't be in for several days."

This information was consistently followed by a long pause before the next, predictable response.

"Do you know where he is?"

"No, I'm afraid I don't. He's gone on a short vacation."

"He didn't say he was going anywhere," the voice would say.

This is where the bachelor's code of honor kicks in.

"Ummm, it was a spur of the moment thing. You know, family stuff."

"Uh huh. But you don't know where he is?"

"No, I'm sorry. But I'd be happy to take a message for you."

"No thanks. When did you say he'd be back?" This question, of course, truly meant what day, what hour, and what second would Mick again be available.

"He'll be back Monday…" Two weeks, one week, or four days, it didn't matter, the response was the same once the information was provided.

"Thanks."

"You're wel…" click.

Once in a great while an actual customer would manage to get a call in.

"Hello, Wynn & Scutter Jewelers. How may I help you?"

"Hi, I'd like to check on the status of my watch repair, please."

"Certainly, may I have your name and ticket number, please?"

"My name is Judy Aldrich, but I'm afraid I've misplaced my ticket."

It's actually quite shocking when someone *does* have the number—truly a rare event.

"I'm sure I can get some information for you." They have no idea, though, that their lack of a claim number transforms me into a human sacrifice to Sherm, the repair god, hunched over his bench and concentrating on a project. Fully aware that he has heard every syllable of the phone conversation from a few feet away, I prepare myself for his abuse, which quickly takes on the semblance of a broken record.

"Sherm, I need to check on a watch repair for Judy Aldrich."

"What's the ticket number?" he asks sternly, without looking up from his work, knowing the answer.

"She doesn't have it."

"No ticky, no laundry," he says.

"But she doesn't have it," I respond, as part of the ritual.

"You'll have to look it up, then."

He loves to make me look it up. The task involves sloughing through a two-inch-thick ring binder with hundreds of barely legible, handwritten entries. After tediously studying page after page, hundreds of names blur until double vision sets in, and finally a scribble barely resembling "Judy Aldrich" is entered with the pertinent information Sherm insists he needs to find the job.

"It's number 5411, a lady's yellow Waltham wrist watch in for an overhaul and a new crystal."

This is when, as Dale always said, "You want to get out the suicide tie." Without ever raising his head and keeping his right hand on the tweezers or screw driver or whatever implement he was using at the time, Sherm would reach way over to his left, as though he had eyeballs in the side of his head, then pick up and dangle the watch from its ticket and string like a pair of dirty underwear. "It's done," he'd say without moving his head one iota, and another customer would be happy.

*   *   *   *

Business always slowed down a bit in the summer. People were on vacation or they were saving all their money in preparation for vacation, or they'd just come back from vacation, all their money spent. Repairs stayed busy, however. Between this store, South Persy, and Alaidon, the jobs just kept pouring in. One thing was sure: if customers didn't have the money to buy new, they made sure to keep their old jewelry, especially their wristwatches, in good repair.

I busied myself for the next few days of Mick's vacation and as time went by, I came to recognize Bernice and Eunice, a pair of Molly's coffee clutch gang. One or the other routinely poked her head in the door and signaled, usually twice a day, and Molly dropped whatever she was doing to disappear for as much as an hour. The trouble with Eunice and Bernice was that I couldn't tell which was which, as they were identical twins. They dressed differently, but everything else was the same: same hair, same glasses, same smile, same everything.

They would visit occasionally with me over the counter or I would bump into one of them on the street, but I could never tell them apart. Only Molly seemed to be able to accomplish that.

With Molly gone for coffee and everyone else preoccupied, the floor was all mine. I prided myself on how efficiently I accepted or delivered repairs, unless doing so involved the ornery one.

"Sherm," I half-whispered so as not to startle him.

"Uh huh?"

"This fella's got a pin needs to be put back in his watch band."

"Got the pin?" Sherm asked, hunched over his bench as usual, face pressed into his work but wearing his meaner-than-a-wounded-bear attitude.

"Yep, right here," I said and smiled, but it didn't help because he never looked up anyway.

"Put it back," he said.

"I tried, but it doesn't go in." I really did try.

"Came outta there, didn't it?"

"Yeah…"

"Then put it back."

"I've tried every way and it won't go," I objected.

"Tried to stay in your momma's belly, too. Didn't think you'd fit there either, I bet."

Eyeballs glaring in the side of his head, Sherm reached over and put what he called his "pigsticker"—a bone handled jackknife—on the counter. "Put it back," he said, face still buried into his work.

Using the pigsticker, I wiggled and wrenched the spring-loaded pin until it seated in the lug, taking care not to scratch the watch case or band. "I got it!"

"Uh huh," Sherm replied with typical enthusiasm.

I retreated without even looking in his direction for fear that a brutal "I told you so" would follow.

*   *   *   *

I spent the days polishing and shining, waiting on the repair trade and watching Bill size rings, re-tip diamonds, and set stones. "Learn a trade," he'd tell me. "You'll always have a job."

The veterans Dale and Molly took care of the sales. I wouldn't have had a clue what I was talking about, so I handled the few engraving jobs we took in and bided my time, waiting reluctantly every morning for Sherm's sourpuss face to darken the front door.

Sure enough, it happened again. Only moments before Sherm's arrival one day, the same tall, ghostly stranger slithered by, the same spooky gaze shooting from the corners of his eyes as he passed. He didn't say a word or make any gesture, just leered as I dropped my head and watched him from under my eyebrows.

Inevitably, Sherm always caught me off guard.

"Must be you been weird in the morning all your life."

Thinking about it, I probably did look rather like a freaked-out pothead, the way I returned the stranger's gaze with a dopey aloofness.

"Sorry," I said.

"Not near as much as me," Sherm sighed. "Think you could manage to hold the door?"

He was carrying a brown grocery bag, folded at the top but obviously very heavy, judging by the way he had to support it on one knee while he unlocked the door. "Being a doorstop shouldn't take too much effort," Sherm mocked.

Oh, man, I thought, *just a few more days until Mick's return.* I concentrated on my responsibilities around the store and made my brief daily excursions to South Persy for a giddy moment with Smelly Nellie.

*   *   *   *

My duties were never routine nor predictable. Standing behind the counter in a jewelry store is similar to tending bar. Few transactions take place without some small talk; sometimes even life histories are related. Most jewelers—and bartenders, for that matter—consider such interaction drudgery, the boring consequences of their business. From the very beginning I always derived a great deal of joy in the personal experiences and histories shared by customers, often an unequaled source of wisdom on life and human nature.

It was Thursday afternoon and I only had one day left before Mick would be back to run interference on my behalf during a Sherm attack. Molly was busy pounding out documents and Dale had left early for an appointment. Sherm was silently tinkering at his bench, and Bill apparently had no metal to forge because a rare hush permeated the store.

No one flinched when the brass bell announced the arrival of a visitor. It was just a kid, young-looking even to me, about 12 years old, with red hair and freckles. The boy was so gangly I doubt he could fight his way out of the clutch of five-year-old schoolgirls. As I approached, he folded his arms on the display case like a little squirt at the candy counter.

"Hi, what can I do for you?"

His response caused me to suck in my breath clear down to my belly button. "May I speak with Sherm, please?" he politely inquired.

The mere mention of Sherm's name elicited fear on my part, usually for my own well-being, but in this case I wondered what torturous, sadistic, cruel being had sent this little twerp of a kid, with such good manners to boot, to confront Sherm, of all people.

"I'm sure I can take care of anything you need, or I can ask him something for you if you would like," I offered, hell-bent on protecting the kid from any humiliation. There was no reason to throw him to the wolves. I even looked across toward the door to see if a gang of bullies was waiting for him on the sidewalk, promising him a bag of chocolate if he could survive their dare by getting within five feet of the ornery cuss.

"No thank you," he squeaked. "I need to talk to him." His vulnerability almost reduced me to tears.

"Wait here just a minute," I instructed as I shot over to Molly's desk in the wrapping room. She stopped typing and looked up at me as I leaned over the desk to whisper, "There's a little kid out here and he wants to talk to Sherm. What should I do?"

She plucked her cigarette from her lips and leaned around me to get a look at the victim. "Send him back," she said. "I don't see any problem."

I was aghast at Molly's cold-heartedness. You always hear how young people make old people nervous, but this was all backwards. Given no alternative, I stumbled back to the counter and sheepishly offered to let the kid back through the gate. I should've snatched Molly's cigarette from her lips and offered it to the boy—as his first and last.

"There he is," I said as I pointed at Sherm after we'd passed the wrapping room and Molly's desk.

"Thank you," the boy chirped as I rushed back to Molly to intervene on his part.

"What should I do?"

"About what?" Molly asked.

"About the kid." She could see the panic growing on my face.

"What the heck are you talkin' about?" she responded, perturbed.

"You know," I said, poking my head in Sherm's direction, "Sherm."

"Look," she'd lost her patience and was squinting at me, "if Greg wants to see his dad, we're not going to stop him."

With those words, my view of the world was forever changed. "*Sherm's...married?*" I stammered in disbelief.

"Well, no. His wife died when Greg was about five. He has a daughter too, just graduated from high school. You didn't know that?"

"*Sherm has kids?*" I uttered in total amazement.

I had planned to watch a child succumb to a violent end, but now I had to see how the demon dealt with his own offspring.

I dashed to the back archway and eavesdropped around the corner with my jaw into a you-gotta-be-kiddin'-me gape. Sherm handed the heavy brown paper grocery bag to his son.

"Is it workin'?" Greg asked.

"Yep, finished it just b'fore work."

Standing next to his seated father, which brought them to approximately the same height, Greg pouted a little and asked, "Aren't you gonna put it in?" his voice tiny and pleading.

"No," Sherm answered sternly, "you put it back."

I couldn't believe his words.

The tiny voice continued, "But I don't know how it goes."

"Come outta there, didn't it?"

"Yeah, but..."

"Then put it back." Sherm placed a handful of screw drivers and wrenches on top of the bag.

"All right," responded Greg in a characteristic tone of aw-shucks adolescent resignation.

Then, for a brief moment, I perceived the corners of Sherm's lips turn into the tiniest smile, his voice softening to a soothing tone, and his head bobbing slightly when he said, "You can do it, Greg."

The lapse was short-lived because in the same breath, his face shrank back into true Sherm form as he stated firmly, "Dinner's at six-thirty. Don't be late."

Greg's smile split freckles from ear to ear as he said, "Thanks, Dad!" and bolted around the counters, through the little gate, and out the door. The brass bell clanged back against the glass as the door swung shut and I stood there, slack-jawed, thinking that this had to be some twisted delusion my brain wanted desperately to believe.

I turned toward the ornery ole watchmaker and smiled. Sherm's eyes revealed that he'd been found out, and a tiny hint of a smile crept across his face before he turned back to hunch over his bench. The silence between us spoke volumes, finally broken by, "Now leave it alone, or you'll draw back a bloody stub." It was muffled, spoken into his bench.

From that point on, while Sherm's scoldings still pierced my ears, they never again packed the same wallop. "You gonna stand there stupid all day, or you gonna get back to work?" He still got my attention, but terror no longer gripped me at the sound of Sherm's voice. I quit standing around looking stupid—then, and for the entire summer. I eventually learned to do quick jobs and simple fixes without bothering Sherm, Bill or Dale. Looking up jobs in the book before asking about them became routine and oddly enough, increased efficiency by about 50 percent.

*   *   *   *

Turns out the automatic pitching machine from Greg's summer sports activities class had broken down. Baseball was his favorite pastime at summer school, where he spent his days while Sherm was at work. His dad offered to repair the clockwork-type mechanism and had worked on it well into the morning hours, but the repair was still incomplete when Greg had to leave for his first class.

No longer feeling so threatened, I didn't have to arrive early anymore to sneak away and hide from Sherm. Besides, his verbal jabs generally had some basis. As a widower solely responsible for his children's support and upbringing, he was destined to parent from a distance at times. He could not be home all day to coddle his kids, and he wasn't about to interrupt his work to coddle me or anyone else either. Sherm had his own special way of getting all of us—children and adults—to straighten up and fly right.

Far from the open book I had originally thought he was, Sherm was a complicated man, deeply affected by the too-early loss of his wife. While he flowed over with joy about anything pertaining to his children, on a personal level he accepted the life he'd been dealt, consigned to his routines. To truly know Sherm was to sense a profound sadness, the product of his longing for the woman he never mentioned, even though he always felt her presence.

PEANUT BUTTER AND DIAMONDS

"There's sandwiches in the drawer!" I proclaimed. The showcases had been dusted, reorganized, and polished to a new pinnacle of gleaming splendor. Dale asked me to go through all the drawers beneath the display cases to reorganize them, too. The first one I opened stored about six plastic sandwich bags, each revealing a sandwich with a bite or two missing. "There's a whole pile of 'em! What the heck are all these in here for?" I exclaimed in amazement.

"Oh, ha, ha, ha, ha," chortled Molly from her desk in her raspy laugh. "Those are mine, but I don't need them anymore. You can toss them."

I looked at Molly quizzically, then bent down and opened another drawer. Sure enough, more sandwiches. "All of 'em?" I asked.

"Ha, ha, ha, ha—yes, all of them."

"She's destined to either burn us out or have us infested with rats. She just hasn't decided which fate she prefers for us yet," Mick said as he passed by, then disappeared again into the wrapping room as Molly lit up a cigarette in response.

"And leave my shoes be," she puffed at me. "I know where they are and I don't want to have to go searching for them."

"What shoes?" I asked.

"In the other draws." She always left the "er" out of "drawer."

I examined the bottom drawers, which were, of course, filled with dozens of pairs of shoes, all jumbled up.

Every day Molly whipped a sandwich out of her purse. She must not have eaten at her coffee clutches, because she nibbled on one of her sandwiches just before or after her get-togethers with the twins. Occasionally, she could be caught chomping away on a sandwich, a bite-sized segment protruding from the plastic bag just as a customer approached.

"I'd like to look at some engagement rings," a well-dressed gentleman said after the clanging of the bell on the door ceased. And there was Molly, a cigarette with an inch of ashes perched between the fingers of one hand and a partially eaten peanut butter sandwich in the other. "I know just what you're looking for," she said as she balanced the butt on the counter's edge, missing the ashtray by about six inches and knocking the ashes to the carpet. Then she rushed, sandwich still in hand, to the showcase near the door where the diamond rings were displayed. She all but grabbed the poor guy's necktie across the counter to drag him down there, peanut butter delight pointing the way.

Then Molly opened the showcase as the steel ball bearing slides made a "clickity, clickity, clickity" sound and examined the contents of the showcase to find the perfect ring the infatuated young suitor needed to bind his promise of love. The process somewhat resembled the mystical manner in which a fortune teller might hone in on a tea leaf during a reading. But who could doubt the wisdom of the expert, as only the most expensive and fabulous piece in the showcase would do? Molly proceeded to pluck the ring from its display and replace it with her half-eaten sandwich.

"This is the ring your sweetheart dreams of," she said. "The *only* one that will do. Your fiancée will have the most beautiful engagement ring she's ever seen!" emoted Molly, locking weepy eyes with her customer. "She'll appreciate that you are the most amazing man she's ever known, and she'll be yours," Molly promised, amused by her own finesse.

"It is nice, isn't it?" dreamily commented the smitten young man as he gazed, goo-goo eyed, at the ring, completely oblivious to the crumbly peanut butter and jelly delicacy now displayed among the lesser diamonds.

"Oh, my," Molly said, her eyes closed and her head swaying like a soothsayer entering a trance, "the moment you put this on her finger, she will never doubt you and she'll follow you anywhere."

"Is it a good diamond?" the customer asked.

"Why, this is one of the finest diamonds you will ever lay eyes on. It is a full three-quarter carats, nearly flawless, and the very finest blue-white color." Weepy eyed again, but transforming from fortune teller to mother, Molly went in for the kill. "Certainly your young lady deserves nothing less."

"Wow!" the young man responded, convinced this was the ring he must have, the ring *she* must have. "But how much is it?" he asked while turning the ring in his fingers to watch the fiery light dance from within the stone.

"It is only $1100.00," Molly revealed, as though describing the cost of a candy bar. Eleven hundred dollars may sound like a bargain for a fine diamond today, but in those days one could purchase a brand new, nicely-equipped automobile for about three times that sum.

The young gentleman quickly turned his gaze away from the stone, his hand darting out to set the ring back on the counter and his arm jerking back to his side as if the jewel had scorched his fingers. Feeling the stress, he tugged at his collar and tie. "Gosh," he sighed, feeling inadequate and defeated, "that's a lot more than I can spend. Do you have something nice that doesn't cost as much?"

This was where Molly excelled beyond all others. Molly sincerely always felt that each and every potential young bride deserved the very finest, so she would go to work on her behalf. "Certainly," she responded, "but you do love this girl, don't you?"

"Of course," the puzzled young man responded.

"What is her name?"

"Nancy."

"Don't you think Nancy should have the best? Don't you think Nancy should always have the best of everything?"

"Sure, but..."

"Now you listen, young man, every woman deserves the best, but they don't often get it. If you truly love her, you'll give her what she dreams about, not just what she needs."

"I know that, but..."

"There are no buts about it. If you can't do that for her, then you have to step aside for the man who will. Do you really want anything less for her?"

The poor soul gingerly picked the ring up again from the counter, a mild look of pain stretching across his face as he calculated the long-term consequences of his impending purchase. The stone sparkled seductively as he admired it. In a last-ditch effort to save himself from financial ruin, he invariably glanced hopefully at the smaller stones beneath the glass, took one look at them sitting next to Molly's peanut butter and jelly sandwich, and succumbed. "Could I make payments?" he inquired.

"Now there's the man Nancy wants to marry!" Molly exclaimed, boasting a huge smile of victory for her fellow female.

The young lover slapped his $300 deposit on the counter—far more than he had intended to spend—and signed up to make installments on three times more. Feeling simultaneously defeated and triumphant, the young man proudly strutted out the door, appearing taller than when he had arrived.

More than just a shrewd businesswoman, Molly was a true romantic. She wanted every groom-to-be to realize the virtue of commitment. While they typically intended to devote a paycheck or two and perhaps a tax return or bonus for the ideal ring, they would end up clearing their calendars of beer nights with the guys after Molly finished with them. If good habits take hold early in a courtship, then Molly was responsible for helping mold many a frugal, conscientious provider. This same scene played over and over again in the store.

*   *   *   *

As I filled one wastebasket after another with brick-hard sandwich remnants, I realized that each one was a trophy. Instead of finishing a sandwich after a sale, as I had assumed, Molly neatly rewrapped it and deposited it in the nearest drawer, like a hash mark on a pistol grip. Each one marked a new engagement, a special anniversary, or a romantic holiday. With regularity, magnificent diamonds, beautiful rubies, and elegant watches cunningly traded their places in the shop with stale peanut butter sandwiches.

*   *   *   *

I came to appreciate Molly's true intentions for selling jewelry while working during a Christmas break from school. She would later illuminate the convoluted details of the situation that transpired, explaining that the man she'd waited on was Bernice's husband.

As mentioned previously, Molly's friend Bernice was one of the indiscernible twins in the ladies' daily coffee clutch. A fellow female and trusted friend, Bernice had returned to the workforce after raising her two children. With the children grown and on their own, she thought she could enhance her marriage by working outside the home to help improve the lifestyle she and her husband had shared for many years. Unfortunately, Bernice was married to a man who, until recently, Molly had only suspected of being a "conniving letch and unfaithful jackass."

Molly had apparently seen the couple together on occasion, and she learned through the coffee clutch that they were husband and wife. While she recognized Bernice's husband as a steady customer who purchased a considerable amount of rather exquisite and expensive jewelry, he was unaware of the relationship between Molly and his wife, which was limited to the coffee clutch.

Always the curious romantic, Molly tried for months, once the husband's identity was revealed, to discover the whereabouts of the fancy jewelry. Bernice wore only modest, older pieces and some cheap costume sets that she had purchased for herself, Molly learned. Privately, our jewelry sleuth held out hope that Bernice kept the diamond brooches, pendants, and bracelets purchased by her husband ferreted away for safe keeping, only to wear on special occasions. Molly never failed to comment on each piece Bernice wore, but she never once heard any mention about jewelry that was too nice to wear to work. Dedicated to uncovering the truth, Molly continued her investigation.

About four days before Christmas, a developing snowstorm gave the staff at Wynn & Scutter a reprieve from the crowds of shoppers who were held at bay by the weather. The ding and clank of the bell on the door seemed more pronounced in the absence of shoppers' voices and laughter at the counter.

Serving as short-term holiday relief, it was my responsibility to be ever-present to greet and help customers while the rest tended to their duties off the sales floor, so I quickly moved through the back room to approach the handsome, friendly-looking gentleman who entered. I was enthused to chat with the fellow because he struck me as the embodiment of Santa Claus—incognito. A crown of white hair embellished his head while a neatly trimmed white mustache and beard adorned his upper lip and chin. I half expected him to whip open his coat to reveal a red suit over black boots.

As I passed through the wrapping room and by Molly's desk on my way toward the front of the store, I noticed that she was resting with her legs crossed, one arm across her chest and the other propping up a smoking cigarette, her head bowed slightly and her eyes closed. She seemed quite at peace. As I advanced toward the customer, she raised sleepy eyes to see who had entered.

It will never be known whether Molly went around, over, or straight through her desk; I didn't see. But before I could take half a step further, she blocked my path and she actually tamped out her cigarette in an ashtray. With squinty eyes and a somber expression she told me in a decisive, quiet voice, "This one's mine," and she wheeled toward the shopper.

"Welcome and Merry Christmas," she said to the friendly-looking fellow while he stomped snow from his boots.

"Good afternoon and Merry Christmas to you as well," he responded.

"Thank you. What may I help you with on this beautiful winter's day?"

"I'd like to do a little shopping."

"For a lady, I presume?"

"Yes, yes, something special for a lady."

"Did you have anything particular in mind? Or may I offer some suggestions?" asked Molly, sounding like her friendly, helpful self. I wondered why she was so intent on waiting on this particular gentleman.

"I remember some of the lovely pieces you've selected in the past, sir," Molly commented, looking somewhat devious. "I have some wonderful items to compliment them that I'm sure your sweetheart would just love."

"Santa" tickled his whiskered chin for a moment while he ruminated. "I thought perhaps a diamond pendant…"

"Oh, what a splendid idea! She'll be a very happy girl come Christmas morning. But as I recall, didn't you get her a diamond pendant just a year ago?"

This was totally out-of-character for Molly, for as far as she was concerned, every woman should be draped and glistening with diamonds from head to toe— the more the sparkle, the better the man. Molly was clearly fishing for something.

"Well, yes," "Santa Claus" responded, "but she liked that one so much that I thought I might find something a little different so she can trade them off from time to time."

"Your wife is a very lucky woman, indeed. I have just the thing!" she said as she scurried through the tiny gate toward the display cases in the middle of the room. "Right over here," she chirped as she guided her unknowing victim to the showcase. His coat was unbuttoned now, and I was disappointed to see slacks and a beige turtleneck instead of a red suit. They chatted briefly as Molly unlocked the showcase, and completely compromising her penchant for excess, she removed a tiny, conservative diamond-and-gold teardrop on a dainty little chain.

"This is a wonderful little piece," she said, "and only seventy-eight dollars."

The gentleman was as shocked as I was as I eavesdropped from the back of the room.

"Well, er, I was thinking of something a little more spectacular—and more expensive." He surveyed the items in the showcase and pointed to a different pendant. "More like this one," he said, pointing to a three-quarter-inch hand-crafted snowflake encrusted with diamonds to simulate the sparkle of a natural, icy crystal.

"You have exquisite taste," Molly observed as she lifted the snowflake from the case in it's tasteful box. "This half-carat of diamonds would melt any woman's heart. It's only four-hundred and fifty dollars, a bargain for the pleasure it would give." She handed him the box, watching him like a hawk.

"Santa" twisted and turned the box in his hands, then tipped it up to let the chain and pendant rest onto his palm, "Four-fifty you say? Yes, that's it, that's the one. Yes, I'll take this one. It truly is quite beautiful."

"Very good, an excellent choice. She will be very pleased. May I put a nice Christmas wrap on this for you, sir?"

"Oh yes, that would be fine…and save me the trouble," he said, handing the box back to Molly.

Everything seemed normal. Molly seemed like her old smiley, giddy self, and our "Santa" had selected a pricey, elegant piece that I knew was much more to Molly's liking. But everything wasn't normal. Typically, she would have motioned for me to gift-wrap the package while she rang up the sale. Instead, she asked "Santa" if he'd like to fill out a gift card to accompany the package. We had a few near the register for the occasion when someone requested one, but I was told early on that we didn't offer too many "freebies" when we made a sale to control overhead. Here was Molly, breaking the rules again, and I still didn't know what she was up to.

"The card would make this nice and personal," she continued.

"Yes," responded the unwitting victim, "that's a fine idea. I'd like to do that."

"Steve," she finally hailed my attention, "would you please get us a gift card?"

I retrieved one of the fancy little linen note cards and an envelope from beneath the cash register in the wrapping room. I returned and handed the card to Molly.

"Would you like me to wrap that for you?" I asked innocently.

Molly held the boxed pendant in her hand, clenched firmly in her closed fingers. As she turned away from "Santa" to address me, her smile faded to a sly, fiery-eyed glare. "Not yet," she instructed through clenched teeth, "we'll get the card filled out and you can tie it on with ribbon." She turned back to her customer, with a broad smile, and handed him the card and a pen.

I thought for a moment about how to tie a one-and-a-half-inch card to a tiny package with three-quarter-inch ribbon and found myself completely flummoxed. Molly must have read my mind, because as I started to speak, she turned to me, transforming once again from Jekyll to Hyde, and rasped, "It will look better that way!" the look in her eyes signaling me to shut my flap. Smiling again, she turned back to the fellow as he contemplated what to write. "I suggest something romantic," she purred.

"Of course, of course," he muttered as he leaned over the card and scribbled. After sealing the card in its envelope, he handed it and the pen back to Molly. "There we are!"

"Oh, you should put her name on the envelope," she coaxed, winking at him, "to let her know it's just for her."

"Certainly," he conceded, and the envelope and pen passed back and forth one more time.

"Sally," she read out loud. "What a beautiful name. Your wife's name is Sally?"

"Well, er, no, just a close friend."

"I see. Well, as long as you're selecting expensive gifts for women, perhaps you would care to look at something for Bernice, you low-life worm!"

He didn't even flinch, "You know Bernice?"

"Yes I do, and if you think I'm selling you this pendant for your two-bit floozy, you've got another think coming, mister. I believe Sally's enjoyed quite a few perks over the last few years while Bernice has been working a full-time job! Don't you?"

This was no Santa Claus. The fact that he showed no sign of guilt made Molly even angrier. Only the nape of her neck was visible to me now, but it was turning purple. I sure wouldn't have wanted to be the object of her attention at that instant.

"You don't understand," he reached up and snatched the card off the counter to hide it away in his pocket.

"Oh, I understand all right, buster. You've got a loving, hard-working wife—the mother of your children—at home and you're out spending her money on your hussies," Molly fired back. As her fury escalated, Molly's feet, usually in perpetual motion, were glued where she stood, her hands firmly planted to the counter top, still clenching the crumpling pendant box. She was paralyzed with anger.

"I believe I've made a mistake," the Santa imposter mumbled as he turned and quickly walked toward the door without another word, but it was a narrow escape.

Molly traversed the counter, her arms flailing now, the pendant banging around in the box. "A mistake, ha! You've made plenty of mistakes, Herb darling."

Santa's name was Herb. Molly had her ace in the hole. "You'll know what a mistake is when Bernice finds out where her hard-earned money has been going!" she hollered after him.

Herb was lucky that our avenger didn't have a broom in her hand, because she would have beaten him mercilessly about the head all the way out the door. The bell clanged and clanked furiously as Herb fled into the freezing blizzard, oblivious to his unbuttoned coat and the fierce weather outside.

"You'll get yours, mister," Molly hollered into the frigid air after Herb swept out of view.

*   *   *   *

Molly stood gazing through the glass door at the snow being propelled sideways by the wind, the intense flush in her neck subsiding. The pendant would survive the onslaught, but the box, now slipping from her vise-like clutch, would be forever crushed. Turning from the door to pass back through the tiny gate, she quietly proclaimed to herself, "I got the son of a bitch!"

It wasn't until that moment that I realized everyone else had been privy to the spectacle, too. Mick was right in front of me, spying around the wall from the wrapping room, but I'd been so caught up in the drama that I hadn't noticed him. Dale was right behind me, still sitting in his chair, but wheeled into the archway. Sherm was peering over his glasses across the counter by his bench, and Bill was peeking around the corner of his cubicle.

Everyone remained motionless and silent until Molly reached the back of the showroom, surrounded by five sets of eyeballs, watching her in total amazement and wondering what could possibly come next.

"What's the matter with all of you fools? Don't you have some kind of work to do?" Molly inquired as if nothing had happened.

Dale broke the ice, imploring, "Couldn't you have at least gotten his money before you chased him away?"

"Heh, heh, heh," Sherm added.

"Way to go, Molly!" Bill observed.

Mick and I ran for cover in case she wasn't quite through yet.

Molly never told Bernice about her encounter with Herb. We wanted to know why she didn't let him pay for the pendant and keep it to give to Bernice, or why she didn't beat him to the grab for the card and expose to his jilted wife whatever condemning sentiments the envelope contained. But alas, it was not her way.

One of Molly's goals in life was to persistently persuade men to embrace virtue by manipulating them into recognizing their own proper truths. Although gossip was one of her favorite pastimes, tattling to Bernice was against Molly's rules. She had laid the framework for the truth to be revealed in its own time.

The two women remained friends and the incident was never mentioned, but Bernice must have found Herb out, because the two divorced about a year later.

We never saw Herb again, although a changed Bernice—now tied more closely to her twin—poked her head through the door with typical frequency to announce the coffee clutch.

There is little doubt in my mind what caused the deeper worry and frown lines in Bernice's complexion. She became a different person inside and out.

THE BACK ROOM
BOOZER

Christmas Eve morning arrived and I plodded along my usual course from the bus station through the downtown streets toward the shop. The sun peeked over the buildings in the early hours to reveal a vivid blue sky, and the crisp air carried my breath away in wispy clouds. The storm had dissipated the morning after the "Herb" incident, and shoppers frantically ticked off their last-minute lists, preoccupied by thoughts of loved ones and anticipation of the holiday excitement.

Approaching the shop, I saw Sherm round the corner, side by side with the tall, gaunt henchman who had haunted my mornings the previous summer. We arrived in front of the store simultaneously.

"Merry Christmas, Sherm," I spouted, while keeping one eye on the ghostly-looking giant. My greeting elicited an uncharacteristic smile and response from Sherm.

"Merry Christmas!" he beamed back.

My seasonal greeting to the stranger did not reap the same response. Drawn and stoic-looking as usual, his face conveyed a weighty sadness. "Happy holidays," he almost whispered in a husky monotone and turned toward his regular destination.

"You know that guy?" I inquired of Sherm as we entered the store.

"Uh huh."

"He works downtown?"

"Uh huh."

"You know his name?"

"Uh huh."

"Oh, come on!"

"That's Sonny."

"Uh huh." My mimic drew a nasty look.

"People don't take to Sonny much. He can be a bit testy."

Takes one to know one, I thought. "Where's he work?"

"Owns the Gem Market. That's ole 'Show Me the Cash' Sonny."

"Whaddaya mean, 'Show Me the Cash'?"

At last some answers, but Mick wandered out of the wrapping room to see who was invading his quiet engraving time, readying for some last minute pick-ups. "Mornin' guys. Merry Christmas."

Sherm looked in Mick's direction and pulled his head back a little. "You're lookin' a little haggard this morning, Mick. Have a late one, did ya?" My chance to learn more about Sonny was lost.

"Aw, Shermy…just a little party with the gang. You know."

"Uh huh. She wrapped yer package real nice for ya, did she?"

Mick went on the defensive. "Maggie's been callin' for you."

"Uh huh. Ya know, if you marry one of 'em the decoration gits a little dull, but the presents git better with time."

"So they say, Sherm. So they say."

"Hey," I interrupted. "What about this Sonny guy?"

Sherm nodded his head at me. "He thinks he wants to know about our friend Sonny."

"Yeah!" Finally back in the conversation, I prodded Sherm. "What's this 'Show Me the Cash' thing?"

Relieved at the change in the topic, Mick turned away from Sherm and chuckled. "Markowitz doesn't waste much time, and we figure he's been taken a few times. He gets different customers than we do. If you were to shop at his store and pick something—say a ring—out of his showcase, he'd pat the case with his outstretched hand like this…" Mick offered his imitation, standing at a showcase and gently palming the glass top, "and he'd say, 'Lay the money here and I'll show you the ring.' People say he never smiles and they wouldn't go there if not for the deals he gives 'em. Others say they've seen him run people out of the store just for window shopping."

I tried to picture this ghostly-looking man behind a jewelry case, interacting with customers. "Is he really like that?"

"That's what people say. Sherm's the only one of us who talks to him much; they ride the same bus."

That explains why they always show up at the same time. If I hadn't learned about Sherm's secret identity, I might have thought it was something in the water in their part of town. I decided it was best to avoid Sonny and his store completely. "Is everybody in the jewelry business strange?" I smiled, and Mick returned the gesture, approving of my astute observation.

Bill and Dale arrived together, while Mick and I were still snickering. Molly appeared in a puff of smoke just behind them.

"Keep that darn pollutant outside where it belongs, Molly!" Bill frowned as he removed his hat and scarf.

"But I'd freeze to death!"

"Good!" he commanded, "What's the difference where you freeze? I'm gonna freeze to death inside! Mick, turn the heat up or I'm catching the first bus home."

Dale threw his hands up in the air, brown bags hanging from both arms. "Merry Christmas, everybody! Glad to see you're all in the spirit. We still have work to do and this is my top crew. Let's get to it."

Christmas Eve day was unlike any other in my experience at Wynn & Scutter. The race was over. The rattle and banging of tools at the benches were gone. The rash of incoming phone calls from shoppers ceased and the incessant outgoing calls to locate and gather needed materials were done. If it wasn't finished by now, it wasn't needed for the holiday. The most amazing thing about this odd crew of people was the professionalism with which they excelled in getting the job done. The pride in their finished product was evident and well-earned. The only one who truly baffled me was Bill. He accomplished the goldsmithing and stone setting with amazing skill and precision, practicing what I would call "old world craftsmanship," settling for nothing less than perfection in every detail of his work. The reason his abilities baffled me so was that I knew how much bourbon he consumed on a regular basis. He had enough of it in the back room to support a distillery.

At lunchtime Bill suited himself up for a stroll out into the cold. He pulled his old black buckle-up galoshes over his shoes, wrapped a heavy wool scarf around his neck and face, buttoned up his long coat, then finally pulled his sheepskin hat over his head and ears so far that the only human feature still showing was a bit of nose and the thick, black-rimmed spectacles he needed to see where he was going. He returned about twenty minutes later, his mittened hand wrapped tightly around the neck of a brown-bagged bottle about the size and shape of his favorite libation.

He disappeared into the darkness of the back room, still bundled up like an Arctic explorer. I looked around at my associates to see if Bill's brown-bagged package would solicit a response, but no one flinched. The sneaking of an occasional nip must have been too sensitive an issue to elicit snide comments in the shop, I figured.

One of the first things I checked upon my return for the brief holiday layover was the condition of the showcase drawers. I had received sound praise the previous summer for the efficient manner in which I had converted the drawers from a peanut butter sandwich wasteland to accurately labeled storage. Molly's dozens of pairs of shoes in the bottom drawers were neatly paired and organized by color, just as I had left them, and seemingly untouched. The upper drawers, however, had already accumulated a new assortment of plastic-wrapped luncheon byproducts.

That summer I learned one of the world's greatest truths: no good deed goes unpunished. The reward for my "fine work" had come in the daunting task of cleaning and organizing the back room, or "dungeon," as I referred to it. The project consumed nearly the entire month of August before I returned to school.

*   *   *   *

Since its inception, the business had already survived the onset of the industrial revolution, two world wars and the Great Depression. In that time, quantities of unused parts, unclaimed customer repairs, and sundry stuff that depression survivors couldn't throw away had accumulated in great heaps. The nine-hundred-square-foot back room had been converted into a sort of tiered warehouse. Twelve-foot-high wooden shelves supported only by two-by-two pine spars reached from floor to ceiling, leaving only about two feet of wiggle space around and between them. Adequate when constructed, perhaps, but additional decades of bearing every knick-knack with some possible future use caused them to bulge so that the slightest touch made them squeak and sway with the threat of collapse.

With every square inch of the shelves consumed by pieces and parts and covered with a substantial layer of dust, the darkness in the warehouse resisted any form of illumination. Flashlights were kept at the entrance to the "dungeon" for anyone who dared attempt a trek to the bathroom on the other side of the room.

Being a typical teenager, I had leapt at the first opportunity to scavenge the dungeon for hidden and forgotten treasure. About mid-summer Mick asked me to locate an electric clock motor. He gave me general directions as to where it could be found, but I detoured to pilfer through row after row of shelves to see what amazing things rested there. To my dismay, I found only clock and watch parts, stacks of worthless junk, and the clock motor I was sent for.

In the furthest, darkest corner, a very small space had been cleared to accommodate a ghetto-style living space. A tiny table shoved against the wall supported a puny bronze-colored refrigerator that whirred and buzzed, trying to suck the dust-laden air through its coils. Half standing on the table and half leaning on the wall next to the refrigerator was a battered old lamp with a crooked shade. I wriggled my way to the lamp and turned the switch to bring it to life. It flickered a bit as if tired and weak, then gained its strength and finally threw out all of its twenty-five or so watts to shed light on an amazing sight.

A crudely fashioned, seven-foot tall cabinet, obviously designed to rest against a wall, was positioned—free-standing—at a ninety-degree angle to define the space, hovering precariously like the shelving units in the rest of the darkness. I resolved to watch my footing more carefully as I approached it, as a single trip and grab and I might never be seen or heard from again, left to rot with the rest of the warehouse contents. The remaining space was pretty much consumed by a wicker rocking chair and a five-gallon bucket. The ancient chair's stuffing oozed out of every seam and tear in its cushioned seat and back, and its once-white wicker arms and foundation now slept under the charcoal veil that covered the rest of the room. The bucket rested upside-down to serve as an ottoman.

I set myself down in the chair, nestling into the relic like a foot easing into a familiar, broken-in tennis shoe. As the cushion crackled and the wicker squeaked, my body slid into a pre-fitted, ergonomically perfect napping position, I propped my feet on the bucket and closed my eyes. I was prevented from nodding off by one of two things: either a primordial instinct for self-preservation alerted me to the masses of accumulated crushing stuff looming around me or I was like a little kid who'd been sent alone to retrieve something from the deepest reaches of a dark, damp basement, keeping watch for monsters at every turn. No matter whether the fear was real or imagined, I felt certain that the boogeyman had waited all my life for me to nod off at this moment so he could flick his pinky against the tottering shelves in his own little game of dominoes, leaving me splattered beneath the rubble as the grand finale.

Completely self-absorbed and alert, I decided to commence my investigation of the premises with the contents of the wall unit next to me. The upper half had three shelves, each supporting a variety of tools and wood boxes. Most of the tools were like Sherm's, but laden in the same heavy dust as everything else in the room. Some stored implements like those I had seen Bill work with from time to time. Next, I reached over to lift aside the green curtain that hung across the bottom half of the unit, aiming the flashlight beam with the other hand. I couldn't believe the contents! Two shelves hid at least a dozen bottles of good ole Jim Beam Distilled Kentucky Bourbon, none of which contained more than three fingers' full of booze. Shocked, I rearranged the curtain just as I had found it, leapt from the chair, grabbed the motor, snapped off the lamp, and fled to find truth in daylight.

"Who the heck's got all the booze in the back room?" I unhesitatingly asked Mick, the only person who knew everything about everything. I knew it wasn't his, because he rarely spent any time at all in the back room and the only libations I'd heard him speak of were beer and fruity potions served by a bartender. Somehow I knew he wasn't the back room bourbon type of guy.

"You didn't mess with it, did ya?" he queried, his eyebrows raised.

"No. I didn't touch it, I just found it."

"Good. That's Billy's. He's pretty protective of it. That's his private stash."

"What's it for?"

Mick tilted his head forward and peered from under his eyelids, a condescending technique he'd learned from Sherm for talking to a fool. "Ta drink, you genius!"

Feeling the total idiot as the obvious was revealed to me, I grimaced and walked away. For the next few months, however, I watched Bill like a hawk, looking for signs of "Mr. Morton's disease."

*   *   *   *

Mr. Morton was my old buddy Ben's dad. Good friends, Ben and I had grown up across the fence from each other in the old neighborhood. I was amazed, as early as age five, that Mr. Morton had the cleanest smelling breath of anyone I had ever met; it could cool you off from about twenty feet. The other great thing about Mr. Morton was that he communicated with a five-year-old better than any adult I had ever met. He laughed at all of my jokes, giggling at every word I uttered across the back yard fence. He sang while trimming the flowers along the borders between our properties, and he told great stories, like the one about the time he'd seen a space alien in our back yard. "It glowed like a light bulb," he said, "and it could fly!"

His puffy cheeks glowing red, Mr. Morton bounced in an old steel lawn chair, ice cubes rattling in his glass as he spun his fascinating yarns. Totally captivated,

Ben and I listened, mouths agape, until my parents broke the magic spell, calling me in for bed at eight-thirty, about an hour before the aliens came out.

"It floated across your back yard," Mr. Morton continued, staring at me with dreamy eyes. "The thing was fast. When it came to the fence it saw me standing there. The Martian screamed an eerie, otherworldly sound and flew up in the air, floated over the fence, rocketed past my feet and disappeared..."

Mr. Morton made storytelling high art, and I was enthralled. When I was younger, my dad had mentioned in his kindly, clinical fashion that Mr. Morton was so friendly because he imbibed too frequently. I saw nothing wrong with this, since as a small child, I thought more older people *ought* to go to church and "imbible" more frequently—especially teachers, principals and parents. As I grew older, I slowly became cognizant that there was more to Mr. Morton than a giddy disposition and mouthwash breath.

After the Martian sighting, Ben confided in me that his dad "saw things." "He's a boozer," Ben told me. "He's got bottles hidden all over the place. I used to find 'em and dump 'em out till he caught on. Didn't make any difference anyways, he's always got more."

The Martian turned out to be a neighbor's cat some hooligans had caught and somehow decked out in Fourth of July sparklers. The cat, we heard later, managed to survive the torture with some minor burns but suffered significant loss of hair. The pranksters were caught and I suspect they also experienced a significant loss of hair. Mr. Morton continued describing his encounter with the Martians for about another year.

It's sad when you stop laughing with someone and begin laughing *at* them. I pretty much lost my regard for Mr. Morton one day when Ben and I came home from school to feed his fish. I never considered fish in an aquarium to be pets, but Ben did. Unfortunately, they didn't fare as well as the neighbor's cat. Ben found out that his dad decided he didn't want to drink alone, so he dumped a fifth of vodka into the tank to see what a drunken fish would do. They floated.

*   *   *   *

For the remainder of my summer at the store I made it my personal goal to catch my new boozer in the act. My purpose was not to expose him or to be cruel, as the existence of the spirits appeared to be common knowledge. Since the experience with Mr. Morton, I just had an aversion to being taken in by the ramblings of a sot ever again.

The task proved insurmountable. Although the elements were in place—the illicit den, the stash, Bill's daily indulgence during lunch, and his subsequent singing or humming while he worked—just like Mr. Morton trimming the flowers, Bill was too quick for me. Enthralled with the instruction and direction Bill offered, I listened intently to his stories of "the old days." "Don't be too quick to change things," he would say. "People always want to change everything, even if the changes aren't any better. The true definition of 'modern,' if you ask me," grumbled Bill, "is really nothing more than 'cheaper, faster, and almost-as-good.'"

I waited endlessly, it seemed, for the telltale sign of sterilized bourbon-breath, but even at two feet, all I could detect was the scent of peanuts. Molly carried the scent into the shop, spread between two slices of soft white bread, stuffed in a plastic bag and squirreled into a drawer. Bill carried in fresh-roasted peanuts by the pound, straight from the nut store down on the avenue. He always kept a bag next to his bench. Every once in a while he would set his tools down, shuck a few morsels from their shell, pop them into his mouth, and return to his work, humming and smacking his lips.

Occasionally I would sneak up on Bill after he scurried back to his "den" for lunch. Frustrated, I only found him rustling a sandwich or apple out of a brown paper bag, or sound asleep, feet propped comfortably on the bucket. "Too slow and too late," I'd think to myself.

For weeks I fumbled around in the darkness of the dungeon, gathering and sorting pieces, parts, and junk. The junk outweighed the pieces and parts by about ten to one and Dale had to hire a garbage man to remove two dump trucks full of accumulated worthless stuff. As the tiers of junk came down and light started to filter through the stale dark air, some interesting finds started showing up through the dust.

Most of the salvageable items on the shelves were just odds and ends—parts for clocks, parts for watches, parts for jewelry, and parts for equipment. To put the enormity of the job into perspective, I actually found an entire intact piano amongst the debris! Dale remembered being told about the instrument when he purchased the business, but the warehouse had been so overloaded that it hadn't surfaced in almost thirty years!

At first I thought I'd come across an odd-looking antique parlor table. Given its shape, the object seemed more inclined to belong in a billiard hall than in a music hall. I'd never seen a square piano before, actually flat and rectangular, almost like a massive desk with a keyboard. Standing back, I admired the finely crafted legs, decrying the weight they supported. It wasn't until I wiped the thick dust away from the top and discovered the lid over the keyboard that I realized what this piece of furniture actually was.

I took off at a gallop, practically screaming with glee, to the front of the store and proclaimed my find, and everyone followed me back through the mine field of junk to have a look. Sherm arrived first and seemed keenly unimpressed. Such "extras," I sensed, had always been beyond his modest means. "It's nice," was all he said, examining it. He retreated back to his bench.

Bill took a much sharper interest in the instrument. "That's a beautiful thing!" he observed, smiling while his fingers ran over the smooth woodwork.

We pushed more of the dust away and followed the intricately detailed ribbons of inlay that meandered around the top. We were both "oohing and aahing" as Molly's voice popped up behind us. "Oh, that ole thing," she said, staring at it.

"What?" Bill was a little put out, "You don't think it's amazing?"

"You wouldn't think it was so amazing if you had to spend hour after unforgiving hour at it as a child. Nobody wanted it. That's why it's here, but nobody had the heart to get rid of it either. Now I suppose Jody will put it in his living room. Marsha will just love that!"

Bill and I stepped back up to the instrument to admire it just a little more. I raised the lid and tapped a few keys. Neglected pianos laden with thirty years of dust sound less than heavenly, but the tinkle was enough to draw a tear to Molly's eye. Peeking back, I noticed her wipe a memory from her cheek. If the tear wasn't for the piano, perhaps it was for the memory of the person who had spent all those hours looking over her shoulder while she practiced.

Even more treasures surfaced. Two more watchmaker's benches, one painted white, the other a beautiful combination of cherry and maple were buried in the rubble. My favorite find, however, which was no surprise to anyone else, was an antique cash register roughly the size of a Volkswagen. At least it seemed to weigh that much to me.

Nearly three feet long and a foot-and-a-half deep as well as tall, it sported a great handle—like on a slot machine—on one side. The behemoth lay hidden beneath the great oak door Dale had replaced when he took over the business. The first two changes he made were to replace the cumbersome oak door with a lighter weight aluminum-and-glass model and to replace the brass-and-marble monstrosity before me with a sleeker, smaller, automatic cash register.

The original—a true relic—had been in continuous use at the business from 1917 until its retirement in 1974. I fought against the beast with all my weight and strength to slide it fifteen feet. Every once in a while, especially when one of the newfangled cash registers broke down and had to be replaced, I sneaked back to punch a few of the comfortable, lozenge-shaped keys to see numbered plates pop up in the window. I pulled the great arm and listened to the clackity ratcheting sound as it rotated toward me. The drawer slides smoothly opened and a brass hammer struck a tiny bell with a pleasing little "ping." Nope, they sure don't build 'em like they used to.

For days I continued sorting, tossing and tearing down tiers of junk until the room was finally cleared of every disposable object. About four times the size it originally appeared when I began my task, it reminded me of a dance hall—a huge, open room without any supports—but the perimeter was stacked high with all the usable clutter that I was warned not to toss. The den of deceit in the back corner was exposed and brighter, but it remained untouched.

I was sweeping some of the last remnants of dust and dirt from the floor when Bill walked through to his den and removed a brown paper lunch bag from the little refrigerator. "Why don't you stop stirring up that dust for a few minutes and have some lunch? Vi made an extra sandwich today and I can't eat it all."

"I really should keep working till I get it done," I answered, thinking that as with Mr. Morton, avoidance might be my best strategy.

"Look, if you keep throwin' all that pollutant in the air I'll have to breathe it and eat it right along with my lunch. My wife is a great cook and I'd hate to ruin her delicious handiwork—it's roast beef with a great big slice of my own home-grown sweet onion. Whaddaya say?"

I strongly considered excusing myself and heading down the avenue to Jimbo's for a cheeseburger and fries, but my curiosity got the best of me. What better way to get to the truth than to witness Bill's lunchtime ritual first hand? Would he chug from the bottle or rattle it with ice cubes in a glass like ole' man Morton? Besides, I love roast beef, even if I wasn't convinced about the slab of onion.

Bill walked across the room to retrieve a bucket I'd been using to haul junk. He carried it back and set it upside-down near his own impromptu foot stool. He settled his thick, still-aproned frame into the old wicker chair that creaked and moaned as he sighed and propped his feet on the stool. I hesitated, but leaned the broom against the wall and strode over to rest myself on the dusty bucket.

Bill rattled his way into the brown bag and pulled out two perfectly wrapped sandwich-shaped parcels. Each was meticulously packaged in wax paper, the creases and folds befitting an expensive gift. "Here," he offered, "you take the bigger one; it won't show on you like it will on me."

I carefully unwrapped the sandwich while Bill did the same, ritually peeling back the airtight bundle that was magically secured without the use of tape or string. I remained quiet until I exposed my present. "Wow, homemade bread!"

"Yep," he smiled, "Viola doesn't let me eat much that isn't created with her own hands."

"Really?" I said in amazement, admiring the sandwich as I raised it to take my first bite. My teeth sank into the crusty moist bread, then into a thick slice of crisp onion and an equally thick slab of tender roast beef—the best I've ever tasted. Bill wasn't kidding; Vi was a great cook. And the onion was by far the sweetest and most wonderful ever.

"So, whaddaya think?"

"'Bout what?" I sputtered, my mouth full of delectable ambrosia. I was afraid to ask. Trying to read between the lines, I figured "Whaddaya think" meant, "Think you want a snort to wash that down?"

"'Bout the sandwich."

"Oh!" man, was I relieved. "It's even better than you said. This is really, really good!"

"Yup, Vi's a good cook. I told her what you were doin' back here and she figured you'd get hungry. That's why she made the extra."

"Gosh, that was awful nice. Please tell her 'thank you' for me."

Bill smiled and nodded.

The dialogue was open now. Safe for the moment, I figured direct confrontation might be the best way to get to the truth. I would ease toward my primary target by starting with the tools on the top shelves, then work my way down to the booze.

"So," I said between huge bites of roast beef with home grown sweet onion, "What're all those tools up there for?"

Bill looked up at the shelves like he'd never seen them before. His eyes surveyed them top to bottom, then, looking at his sandwich, he confided, "Those were supposed to be for my boy, Christopher." He didn't look up.

"You mean he doesn't want 'em any more?"

"He might want them, all right, but he can't ever use 'em. Chris is severely handicapped. He's the reason I'm here. I figured Dale might 'a told you."

"No, I'm sorry. He never said. I didn't know. But I don't understand, why is that the reason you're here?"

"I had my own store, you know."

"No, I didn't know that either."

"Oh yeah, I had a real nice place: the Jewel Clinic in Kalamazoo. The Clinic was a good business. I had plenty of my own work and other businesses brought plenty of their repairs to me on top of it. That's how Jody found me. He heard about me, came down to see me. Told me if I ever got tired of working for myself I had an open invite to come up here and work any time. That's about when Christopher was born. Looked just like 'is ole pop."

"But he was handicapped?" I inquired.

"No. No, he was a perfectly normal healthy little boy."

"What happened?"

"When he was three he contracted equine encephalitis. He was very very sick. The doctors told us he wouldn't live to be five."

"Equine encephalitis? I don't know what that is."

"From a mosquito bite."

"Huh?"

"The mosquito carries the disease. Young children are most susceptible. The fever caused severe brain damage."

Bill offered me some milk he was pouring out of a small thermos. "It helps settle that onion into your belly."

"No thanks, Bill, I'm fine, really." I wasn't wondering so much about the bourbon any more.

"I closed the Clinic and we moved here so Chris could be closer to the doctors he needed. I just walked in here with my tools one day years ago and Jody put me right to work. S'been good for Chris. We beat all the odds. He's about your age now."

"Gosh Bill, I'm sorry. I didn't know."

"Nothin' to be sorry about. We've got it pretty well worked out. Keeps Vi busy day and night, but Chris is happy and he's doin' fine."

I stared down at my sandwich silently while I finished it. I looked over at the green curtain hiding the bottom of the cabinet, then looked back up at Bill. He'd laid his head back and fallen sound asleep.

My eyes went back to the curtain and I thought about the contents within. Bill wasn't seeing Martians and he wasn't poisoning kids' pets. Inadequate to judge a man such as this, I quietly raised myself off the bucket and walked through to the front door. Fresh air would do me good. If that kindly gentleman wanted to take a drink now and then, so be it.

I finished organizing the back room and my summer of gainful employment at about the same time. We all said our good-byes—no big deal. Except for Sherm. He smiled, that is, until he learned I'd be back for the holidays.

*   *   *   *

It was Christmas Eve, the five o'clock hour was quickly approaching. Dale asked Mick if he wanted to get things rolling and Mick agreed. I had no idea what "things" were going on, but the anticipation seemed to make everyone happy. Mick made a phone call and shortly afterward a young waitress from the City Pub appeared through the front door. She carried a tray of empty glasses, a large bowl of ice cubes, and several bottles of carbonated beverage.

"Hi, Suzie," Mick greeted the waitress at the counter.

"Merry Christmas, Mick...We're all waiting for you when you're done here."

"I'll be there, Sooz, but I've gotta give Billy a ride home first."

"See you there," she smiled, spinning to fly out the door.

About the time Mick deposited the tray on the counter near Sherm's bench, Bill bounced out of the back room with an unopened fifth of bourbon. Following everyone else's lead, I took a glass from the tray, added a few ice cubes, and waited as Bill walked around the room to pour a generous portion in everyone's vessel. Mick, in turn, served soda water or ginger ale to everyone's liking.

When the glasses were topped off, Uncle Dale stepped forward to offer a toast of gratitude for everybody's loyalty and hard work. "It was a good year," he told us. "My first full year at the helm and I really couldn't ask for a better crew. You should be proud of a job well done."

At that we raised our glasses before trying to down the bubbly liquid. Having turned eighteen in October, I had swallowed a few Slo Gin Fizzes and Mai Tais, but this was a man's drink and it made my eyes water a little. When Dale handed envelopes to each of us, I followed the others' lead by slipping it straight into my pocket.

We drank and talked and laughed, but no one laughed as much or as loud as Bill. He became more giddy with every sip.

By the time Molly, Sherm, and I had finished our brew, Mick and Dale had already poured and swallowed seconds. Bill still had nearly half a glass left, but his nose and cheeks were as red as his fire-forged metals and he was beginning to wobble in his chair.

"What do you think, Billy? Time to go home?" Mick asked as he walked over to Bill's cubicle.

"Yoohoo, Merrrrrrry Chrissmassss! Yep, you bet. Jes' led me git my code and hat," Bill said as he stumbled, one hand feeling the wall as he worked his way to the back room.

He came back out about ten minutes later, with unbuckled galoshes, an unbuttoned coat, a scarf dangling over his collar, upturned on one side and tucked inside the coat on the other, his sheepskin hat balanced precariously on his head. "Les co," he mouthed with over-exaggeration, laughing some more.

Armed against the cold in his coat and mittens, Mick rushed over to Bill's side for ballast. "Think you can make it to my car, Billy Boy?"

"Shurr I can," Bill garbled, pointing a limp arm out into space. "Jes leeead the way."

Mick had trouble gaining momentum. With every step Bill took, he leaned harder on Mick and slowly started to sink. "Somebody give me a hand?" implored Mick.

As I hurried to support Bill on the other side, he looked at me and started sinking in my direction, his weight apparently shifting in whatever direction his face turned. "Merrry Chrisssmasss," he slurred, sweetly.

We guided Bill past his cubicle and down the incline at the archway, all three of us hootin' because his laughter was contagious.

"Does he always get this way when he drinks?" I asked.

"Yep," said Mick, shaking his head.

"After just one drink?"

"Yep, that's our Billy."

Bill burst into song. "Woo hoo, Vi's magin' roz' beef for dinner, tha's what we're havin' tonight."

"How come I've never seen him like this before?"

"You've never been here on Christmas Eve before."

"I don't get it, he drinks all the time, doesn't he?"

Bill kept singing, "Vi's magin' roz' beef, Vi's magi'n roz' beefff."

"Billy's just about the biggest tea-totaler of all time—only takes a drink on Christmas Eve. One evening a year he lets his troubles slip away."

"Then what are all those bottles in the back room?"

"Vi's magin' roz' beef. Mick's stayin' for roz' beef," chimed Bill.

"Thanks, Bill." Mick gently responded, "but I'm gonna meet the gang back here at the pub." Then turning back to me, Mick continued, "The bottles in the back room are the leftovers from every year Bill's been here.

"Yep, Crissssmas," Bill struggled to stay with the conversation."

"He keeps them like trophies."

"Geez, do I feel stupid. I thought he was an alcoholic."

"Vi's magin' roz' beef," Bill crooned, giving his little tune a seasonal touch, "roz' beef roazin' on an ooooopen fire, Jack froz' nippin' ad my noze..."

"*Work*aholic maybe," Mick corrected me.

We reached the car parked at the curb. Mick opened the door with his free hand and we tried to guide Bill gently into the car, but he decided to dive sort of head first. It took a lot of wiggling around to get him seated forward in the little compact with bucket seats and untangled from his coat and scarf. "Les go, roz' beef's waitin,'" Bill sang on, contentedly.

Mick closed the car door as a muffled, muddy rendition of Jingle Bells rang out from the passenger seat. We were shaking hands when his charge beckoned, "...oh whad fun id izss to ride...Aye Mick, lez go. Izss cole' as a packin' 'ouse in 'ere."

"Oh boy, that drink didn't warm him up enough! Gotta go. See ya!"

"Merry Christmas, Mick!" I laughed. A new verse of Jingle Bells had already begun by the time he reached the other side of the car. It got louder briefly when he opened the door. Mick started the engine, and I could hear a faint duet as they drove off and rounded the corner.

I stepped back inside the store to find the other three revelers waiting, and Sherm shoved my coat at me. "What's yer hurry?" he asked.

As I zipped up, we all hollered a greeting to whoever was manning the security system and we stepped back out into the cold.

✶   ✶   ✶   ✶

I learned two powerful lessons during my brief experiences at Wynn & Scutter that year. First, as soon as one begins earning wages, one begins spending about twice as much as one earns. The envelope Dale handed out after the toast was a Christmas bonus. It was generous, but only enough to cover a portion of the purchases I had rung up for Christmas on my new Clay's charge card. Ever one to learn the hard way, I had already cornered myself into having to work the next summer to pay the rest of it off.

Sherm, in his infinite wisdom, didn't have to observe me for long to come to size me up. I was an idiot. The more important lesson, which I didn't learn very well, involved observing people and judging them without really getting to know them.

I bundled up for my walk through the gently drifting snow, plodding across the salted roadways toward the bus depot. Even amongst the locked shop doors and empty downtown thoroughfares, I felt a warmth and a Christmas spirit I hadn't known since I was a little kid. "Yoohoo!" I shouted into the emptiness. "Vi's magin' roz' beef!"

LAUGHTER—THE WORST MEDICINE

The insurmountable stress of my senior year weighed heavily on my psyche. It was a Friday afternoon, and I had to read five pages of a book and do fifteen mathematical equations by Monday morning. In just a month it would all be in the past, and the most I'd have to do for a while would be to enjoy the easy life of an adult—going to work, making lots of money, then going home at night. I needed relief from my burden. A date would do the trick, and laughter would heal all my wounds. Beth could surely provide the cure.

We'd never been out before, or even at a common gathering outside of school, but I'd always been impressed with her happy-go-lucky attitude. Nothing ever got her down.

"Geez, Beth, did you hear? Not one of us in Ms. Dorsham's class got better than a D+ on the test."

"Laugh-laugh, snicker-snicker."

"Geez, Beth, did you know they're talking about canceling spring break to make up for the snow days we had in January?"

"Laugh-laugh, snicker-snicker."

"Geez, Beth, has anyone told you the news yet? The meatloaf we all ate for lunch yesterday was tainted with dreaded toe rot disease. Our teeth and hair are going to fall out and the sickness will cause us all to repeat the year."

"Laugh-laugh, snicker-snicker."

Beth's eyes squeezed closed, her mouth opened wide, and every bouncing freckle laughed right along with her. Approximately the shape and nearly the height of a china Kewpie doll, Beth was the perfect little jocularity machine, topped off with a pretty ribbon in her hair.

I had preplanned the perfect date. Science fiction had finally met its glory days. Aliens looked like real aliens, not like the things Mr. Morton saw running through our backyards. Space ships looked like authentic intergalactic cruisers instead of pie plates whirling around on fishing line, and ray guns look like real weapons that could pulverize an entire universe with a "solitary digit-activated recessing manual response device" or, as we say on earth, "the push of a button." A new outer space spectacular was opening at the mall and we were going to see it, right after plowing through a pizza and pitcher of pop at our favorite senior hang out. All I had left to do was find Beth and ask her out.

"Lose somethin,' Beth?" I asked as I approached her at her locker, rummaging on the top shelf before our last class.

"Steve!" snicker-snicker, "Aw, gawd, I can't believe it!" snicker-snicker, "I've been working on a paper for two weeks. I'm supposed to turn it in next hour and I think I left it at home." She stopped rummaging and turned to me with an open-mouthed, sparkle-eyed smile. "Can you believe it?" Laugh-laugh, snicker-snicker.

"That's a bummer," I sympathized. A sensitive guy, I knew how to be supportive.

"Isn't it though?" Snicker-snicker.

"Hey, you know, I was hoping you'd like to catch a movie tonight."

"Yer kiddin,' right?" Snicker-snicker.

"No, really. I figured I could pick you up and…"

"This is great! Oh, yeah! I know just what we'll see." Snicker-snicker. "It's been playing for weeks and I haven't had a chance to go yet!"

Her face glowed with excitement and her eyes glazed over with a dreamy look as she envisioned whatever flick she had in mind, but I couldn't think of anything playing the last two weeks that I had any desire to see.

"But, I…"

"Oh, yeah! This is great!" Snicker-snicker. "Pick me up at six, the show starts at six-thirty. We can make it in plenty of time." Giggle-giggle.

"But, I…"

"Do you know where I live?"

"No, but I…"

"Here," she turned and rummaged in the locker again to pull out a paper and pencil. "Just take Elm to Oakmont, turn here at Rose Court, and my house is 1809."

"Okay, but I…"

Snicker-snicker. "This is so great! It'll be so much fun!"

"Yeah, but are you sure you don't…"

"Aw gawd, we're gonna be late for class and I don't even have the stupid paper." Laugh-laugh, snicker-snicker. "See you at six?"

"Yeah," I said, suddenly insecure about the date I had planned so well. "See you at six."

I had promised to clean the garage in exchange for the use of Dad's car. My parents agreed, knowing full well the garage might smarten up before I turned fifty. In anticipation of the evening, I swept and polished the inside and outside of the old canned-pea green Vista Cruiser.

If nothing else, I was prompt, and the Cruiser wheeled to a halt in front of 1809 Rose Court five minutes before the appointed hour. With high hopes, I anticipated Beth racing from the house upon my arrival and jumping into my waiting chariot, and that we might forego the dreaded formality of parental inter-ference. I waited. Nothing.

I abandoned the security of the Cruiser and cautiously walked up the skinny path to the front porch of the immaculate little Cape Cod with the meticulously manicured lawn and shrubs, colorful flowers sprouting everywhere. As I stepped onto the porch to ring the bell, a happy-looking man swung the door open before my finger had an opportunity to make contact.

"Hello Steven." Laugh-laugh. "We've been waiting for you."

With a wave of his arm he warmly gestured me into the room. Beth sat on a couch with her hands folded in her lap, and a little girl about ten years of age sat next to her, feet dangling. A woman mirroring the posture of her two daughters sat across the small living room.

"Please come in; I'll introduce the family."

As I stepped into the room, I sensed that either the inquisition was about to begin or I was the evening's entertainment. Hands clasped in their laps, all three stared at me and I didn't know whether to swear to tell the truth and nothing but the truth or to start a little song and dance.

"This is Mrs. Campbell, Beth's mom."

"Hello Steven." Chuckle-chuckle. "So nice to meet you." Chuckle-chuckle, "We've heard so much about you."

Yep, it would be the inquisition.

"You already know Beth, of course."

Snicker-snicker.

"And this is her little sister, Karen."

"Hi Steve." Giggle-giggle.

"Steven," Mrs. Campbell piped in, "we know that Beth was looking forward to your date tonight, but she wasn't aware that her father and I had plans for this evening and she has to be responsible for her little sister. Beth didn't think you'd mind if Karen went along with you to the movie." Chuckle-chuckle.

Laugh-laugh.

Snicker-snicker.

Giggle-giggle.

I sucked it up, big time. "Of course not, that would be fine." Sob-sob.

"Well, it's settled then," Mr. Campbell said. "Beth, take this and see that your little sister gets what she wants at the movie." He handed her a ten dollar bill.

"Okay, Pop." Snicker-snicker.

"And you, young lady, you behave and do as your sister says."

"Okay, Pop." Giggle-giggle.

"I understand your movie starts soon, so you'd better get going."

"Yes," Beth's mom slipped in, "we don't want to ruin your date and make you late." Chuckle-chuckle.

Sob-sob.

We were scooted out the door, snickering, giggling, and secretly crying. It couldn't get any worse than this.

*   *   *   *

We seated Karen comfortably in the back seat of the Cruiser and she was quite taken with the narrow window that cut across the roof above her, or the "vista" in the "cruiser." I played the gentleman and held the passenger door for Beth. By the time I had eased myself into the driver's seat and closed my door, Karen had already propped herself between us, her elbows poking into our shoulders.

"You guys gonna start kissing now?"

"No," I said while Beth snickered.

"You guys gonna be kissing at the movies?"

"No," I replied.

"You guys gonna kissy-kiss good night?" Giggle-giggle.

"*No!*" Beth took over. "Aw gawd, Karen, will you quit?"

"All right. What movie we seein'? Let's see space men."

"Yes!" I responded enthusiastically, actually beginning to like Karen.

"No, Karen, we're going to see a love story," Beth corrected.

"Aw yuk!"

My sentiments exactly.

"Where is this movie we're seeing anyway? We're running out of time; you said it started at six-thirty."

"Let's see space men," Karen prodded.

Go, Karen, go!

"Space men are good for me," I agreed, hopefully, but my desires were instantly stomped.

"It's at the mall, Steve, and you're right, we'd better hurry. Karen, you're lucky to even be coming with us at all. You'll have to be quiet and settle for what everyone else wants to do."

We arrived at the theater with just a few minutes to spare. Beth panicked when we found a line snaking out the door and around the building. It turned out the line was for the new science fiction flick showing in an hour. "Fortunate" to avoid the line, we got our tickets and popcorn and walked right in to a nearly empty showing of Beth's love story.

We seated ourselves girl-boy-girl since Karen would not have anything to do with being next to her sister, and the movie began. Boy met girl, boy liked girl. Girl didn't like boy, and soon boy wasn't sure he still liked girl, and so on. Beth started weeping, but Karen started giggling. I had to choose one emotion or the other, so I stuck with the space men's team.

The more Karen giggled, the more I giggled, and Beth's weeping increased with countering intensity. She finally stabbed her elbow into my arm. "How…" sniffle-sniffle, "how can you think this is so funny?" Sniffle-sniffle.

"Well," I whispered, "he just spent his entire inheritance on that stupid old farm she wants instead of the sailboat." I stifled a giggle.

Sniffle-sniffle. "But she might die without telling him she loves him." Sniffle-sniffle. Beth wiped her eyes with a popcorn-buttered napkin.

"Then all he'll have is the old farm and no sailboat and no money." My seat shook from Karen's quiet laughter, silenced by the shushing of other movie-goers. Beth sobbed louder.

And so it continued—the boy took the girl home to the farm to recuperate from the dreaded toe rot disease or whatever illness plagued her. When he failed to beat the rain to get the crops planted he had to work deep into the night. Getting the tractor stuck in the darkness, torrents of rain engulfed him. The spinning tires dislodged a large rock and slammed it into the back of his head. Just as the boy fell limp from the tractor, coiling and tumbling, lifeless, into a deep, water-logged rut, the tractor freed itself and began to plow in a large sweep back toward the boy.

Along with everyone else in the theater, Beth cried and gripped her seat, wondering if the rising sun would find the young lover planted in the earth like a corn kernel. Unable to stifle her glee at his pathetic misfortune, Karen started in with a new barrage of contagious giggling that had the two of us rocking in our seats with our hands clamped over our mouths.

Moments before the tractor struck, the girl—having sensed something awful from her sickbed—appeared from the bleak darkness, hair and face dripping with rain, her fancy lace nightie coated with mud. She grabbed her true love by his shoulders and dragged him out of the path of the tractor, the tires rolling by his feet with one-hundredth of an inch to spare.

She hunkered over him to shield the rain from his face. The thunder couldn't wake him, the rain couldn't wake him, the roaring tractor couldn't wake him, but when her tears fell on his face while her gentle touch wiped the mud and blood from his forehead, his eyes opened. As the entire theater broke into a sobbing, buttered-napkin-stuffing contest, Karen and I lost it.

"Aw gawd, that's it!" sniffled Beth.

The two gigglers straightened up real fast.

"Let's go," she snapped, totally disgusted with us.

I wasn't sure what to say. "What do you mean?"

Beth leaned across me and whispered firmly to Karen, "Get your stuff, we're leaving!"

"But…" sniff, "it's not over yet."

"It's over for you. I'll come back and see it when you can't ruin it."

"But we're just getting to the best part…"

"Get your stuff!"

I didn't have time to talk her out of it. Before anything else could be said, Beth was ramming her way past my knees to get into the aisle. Karen and I grabbed our stuff and started chasing her out of the theater, following her trail of butter and tear-soaked napkins.

We weren't able to catch her until we made the parking lot. "Where to?" I asked.

"Home."

"It's early. We still have time to get sumthin' to eat or sumthin'."

"We have to go home. It's almost Karen's bedtime."

"No it's not. It's Friday night. I don't have to go to bed till…"

"We're going home, Karen. You have to go to bed."

Karen tried whining, "No I…"

"Shut up! We're going!"

We took our seats in the cruiser and Karen propped her elbows on the seat back again. "Now you guys gonna get all kissy-kissy?" Giggle-giggle.

"Aw gawd, Karen, shut up and sit back."

Karen had a better idea. "Let's get ice cream."

My vote was still with the space men's team. "Hey, yeah, ice cream sounds like a good idea."

Beth obviously felt I'd lost all understanding of the English language, because loudly and very slowly, she said, "We…have…to…go…home!"

The tension on the ride from the mall to Rose Lane was thick with fear as Karen and I fought desperately not to succumb to another torrent of giggles, and our acute awareness of the consequences of another outburst made the task all the more difficult. We did our best, however, and made every effort to distract ourselves by quietly admiring the vista along the way.

When the cruiser pulled up to the meticulously tended little Cape Cod, Beth jumped from the car the moment it came to a stop.

Karen sat still, with her arms folded over her chest and pouted. "I'm not going to bed yet."

"Come on, Karen. Get moving!" The look in Beth's eyes foreshadowed her future as an impatient, intractable mother.

"I'll walk you up to the house," I offered as I pulled on the door handle and started to get out.

"No!" Beth couldn't hide her anger. "No, thank you. We're fine. Thanks for the movie."

I closed my door.

"Yeah," Karen turned to me while she was half-way out the door, "thanks for taking us to the movies." Giggle-giggle.

"Karen…get…in…the…house!"

My voice became weak. "Maybe we can do it again?"

"Yeah," Beth allowed. "Maybe we can do it again. Thanks."

The passenger door thudded shut and Beth turned to follow her little sister up the walk. Through the glass and over the rumble of the engine I heard a faint "Aw gawd!"

The giggly feeling left me, briefly, as I drove away. The night was young and I turned back toward the mall to catch a solo viewing of the new sci-fi flick.

Reflecting on my evening after having been dazzled by the spectacular special effects, three things were clear: young women preferred to watch love stories, little girls preferred to watch space men, and young men preferred to experience a love story or to see space men. Either one would do just fine.

HEY BUDDY, GOT A QUARTER?

June finally arrived and I stepped off the platform, high school diploma in hand, a highly-educated, fully-matured, completely independent and sophisticated man of the world. That's why the first words spoken on my first full day as an adult were, "Hey Mom, can I have a quarter for the bus?"

I had three months to accumulate enough funds to pay for the Christmas gifts I had purchased the previous winter and enough cash to continue my illustrious dating career. Then I'd be off to an institution of higher education to seek my fame and fortune.

My work at the jewelry store drew considerable esteem from my peers, who considered it a prestigious vocation, given the riches associated with it. Little did they know of my little shop or of others like it, however, as ours was the first generation to abandon the city centers for the suburban malls, considering downtown districts nothing but useless antique remnants of past culture.

Little did they know of my little troupe of eccentric "oldworlders" and little did I realize, yet, just how well I fit in.

*　　　*　　　*　　　*

My bus rumbled dutifully on time to deposit its cargo at the station. Uncle Dale charitably offered to have me return for another summer to provide vacation relief for his weary crew. He couldn't possibly have known how I'd been daydreaming for months about returning to watch Bill's torch flame tease the molten metal, to hear all the latest gossip from Molly, to catch up on which Pershing females were vying for Mick's attention, and to find out if I could coax Sherm into assuming a higher opinion of me.

As I stepped from the bus on a perfect Michigan summer morning, the streets of downtown Pershing welcomed me back. The aroma of bacon and eggs from the diner around the corner wafted through the air, and the sweet scent of cinnamon rolls baking a block away competed heavily to stir the hunger of passing crowds. Most would not stop, their bellies already full of oatmeal or crispy flakes chock full of essential nutrients. Some could not stop, having a standing date with their company's time clock. Others would slow their pace to breathe in the airborne flavors of the kind of homestyle cookin' found only away from home. Many, such as myself, could only linger briefly, barred from the feast by a pane of glass and a shortage of pocket change.

Forty minutes early for my own date with a time clock—fondly known as Sherm—I decided to wander and see what was new and what was old. The first block was the same as on my first day of work one year before. The old empty movie theater's marquee loomed over the street, its three-dimensional figures carved into the stone watching me and dozens more as we strolled past. The ghost-aroma of buttered popcorn still won out over the fresh, sweetly baked rolls a few doors down. Across the street the women's apparel shop windows displayed plaster ladies with broad smiles, proclaiming their pride in the fancy clothes they wore. Hats with brims the size of small umbrellas shaded their pasty faces from the morning sun. The bright oranges, yellows, and lime green of their attire lent a festive atmosphere to the early hour.

Clay's room-sized display windows featured furniture, fashions, toys, and all the newest appliances with the most modern conveniences, like a new-fangled toaster oven called a "microwave." Even the fondue pot I'd gotten Mom for Christmas was on display. I hadn't even paid for it yet and it was already shoved way back in one of Mom's highest cupboards and forgotten. I moved on.

My window shopping came to a halt in front of the next building on my walk. One of the numerous jewelry storefronts was vacant! The showroom was empty, the lights that had made the glistening contents of its showcases dance for thousands of shoppers were dead, and the sign was gone. The only reminder of the business was a handwritten notice on the glass door that read, "Come see us at our new, beautiful location in the Pershing Mall!" This shop was the first of many brave soldiers to fall.

I retreated. The cinnamon rolls kept assaulting my senses anyway, and if I was drooling as I met Sherm at the front door it would just set him off for another summer of fun. So I gave myself a few more minutes and plotted my course toward a little park by the river on the edge of downtown.

*   *   *   *

As I rounded the corner to escape the temptation of bacon, eggs, and bakery goods and the specter of the abandoned store, I spied Weasel Will digging through a trash can.

We didn't really know his name; Mick named him "Weasel Will" for his appearance rather than for his demeanor. Weasel Will always wore a derby hat with the brim cocked "just so." The hat was stained with dirt and sweat, and the shiny satin ribbon that once accented the crown now blended into the worn, mottled black and gray felt. Will's arms seemed to jut out almost perpendicular to his frame; his body was so huge it looked as though he hustled up to an air pump every morning to reinflate his bulbous torso. His shoes, always about six sizes too large, slapped the ground like a clown's when he waddled, thrusting one foot in front of the other, and a long topcoat always covered him from shoulder to shin. I wanted to name him "Penguin Pete," but instead Mike dubbed him in honor of his single-most distinctive physical attribute: his face.

Weasel Will had a skinny little face on a tiny little head that was propped between the derby and the coat. A huge, sharply pointed nose divided his face and separated his beady little eyes, making them appear to poke out of the sides of his head. The fact that he had no teeth and his chin just about swallowed his nostrils accentuated the weasel likeness.

One day the previous summer Will had waddled his way into our little shop. "Ding…clank…slap, slap, slap." Molly was out on a gossip tour, and Mick and Dale peered from their vantage points to see who'd arrived. They eyed each other, looked at me, then agreed in unison, "This one's yours," and settled back into their work.

I approached the man with a shameful aversion, but since this was my job, I had no choice but to assist him. I'd seen him in the streets and Mick and I had made fun of him behind his back. Now he was to be confronted.

Weasel Will stood at the watch cases, his arms poking out to the sides and his hands resting on the edge of the glass. His body swayed back and forth while his eyes flicked right and left, examining the showcase contents.

"Good morning. May I help you, sir?"

Silence. His eyes kept flicking and winking at the cases.

"May I show you something?"

"Yep, yep, yep," he snapped, swaying and never looking up, just continuing to flick those eyes at the watches.

"Is there one you'd like to see?"

"Wind it. Wind it," he urged, his head down but his right hand making the motion of winding a watch against his left coat sleeve.

Somehow I had always thought that this dirty creature would stink to high heaven, but the only aroma I detected was the sweet scent of cigars that reminded me of fishing trips with my dad.

"Most of our watches are battery operated now," I said, trying to engage Will. "You don't have to wind them and they are much more accurate."

"Wind it. Wind it," he repeated as he motioned against his sleeve again.

I decided to use the Sonny approach, "You know, the type of timepiece you're asking for will cost at least sixty dollars."

"I wanna wind it," he responded, pointing to a 14k yellow gold, high grade manual-wind watch. Out of over two-hundred watches on display beneath the glass in front of him, only a handful were not battery operated. Will picked one of these out of the crowd.

I reached into the case and selected a much more modest piece, a yellow gold-plated quartz watch with a dial similar to the 14k model. "This one's only forty-five dollars. It's shock-proof, it takes a battery, and you don't have to wind it."

Will's one eye winked at the watch in my hand as his other eye blinked at the one he'd selected. Back and forth his head swayed, eyes flicking at one, then the other.

"I wanna wind it," he said, pointing to the expensive model, then "winding" his sleeve.

I saw no harm in letting Will wind the watch. He couldn't damage it, and there was no chance of him outrunning me if he decided to abscond with it. I put the quartz watch back, reached over, pulled the boxed watch he admired from the showcase by its open lid, and set it on the counter in front of him. His eyes flickered faster and he caressed the crystal with his fingers, "Wind it," he said, still without raising his head.

I pulled the watch from the box and removed it from the sleeve to let him wind it.

Will reached under his left coat sleeve, pulled an old steel watch off over his wrist and hand, and placed it on the counter. I could see scratches and dents on the case and air bubbles floating around in rusty water under the crystal.

Ever so gently, the old man grasped the new watch, slid it cautiously onto his wrist, slowly and methodically wound the stem forward and back between his thumb and forefinger, then raised his wrist to his ear to hear the soft clicking of the winding ratchet. When the winding ceased, his wrist remained propped at his ear to listen for the rhythmic drumming tick-tick-tick.

He listened carefully, eyes watering but still winking down at the showcase, "How much?" he asked.

"One hundred-seventy-five dollars," I read on the inventory ticket on the bottom of the box, "plus tax."

Will listened to the steady tick-tick-tick for a moment longer before unbuttoning the top half of his coat under which he wore a quilted vest. He then unzipped his vest, revealing a flannel shirt, long john-style buttoned underwear, another shirt, and finally worked his way down to yet another vest with pockets.

Geez, I thought to myself, realizing that Will's size was just an illusion, *Bill would love this outfit!*

Will reached deep into a vest pocket to pull out three mangled cigar butts and set them on the counter. He reached in again, pulled out a small coil of string and placed that on the counter, followed by a little ball, a rattling metal throat lozenge box, and a spool of thread. The last thing to come out of the pocket was a tightly rolled wad of bills, larger than a soup can, encircled by several rubber bands.

I stood speechless as Will loosened the bands and peeled out a one-hundred dollar bill, a fifty, a twenty, a ten, and two ones. He had the tax figured exactly. My heart skipped from the sight of all the money. I could swear I glimpsed a bill with three zeroes in the corner…

As I wrote out Will's bill of sale, he stuffed the roll back in his vest pocket, then returned everything else he'd deposited on the counter in the exact order it was removed. Finally, the old steel watch went in with the cigar butts. By the time I'd finished writing, he was re-zipped and re-buttoned and the watch box was being stuffed into an outer coat pocket. By the time I reached out to hand Will his receipt he was already slapping his way toward the door.

"Thank you, sir," I called out after him.

Silence. "Slap-slap-slap, ding…clank."

*   *   *   *

Weasel Will looked exactly the same as I approached him now, digging elbow-deep into the trash can. He pulled something out, winked at it, tossed it back in, and dug deeper pulling up a foam coffee cup with a lid fitted to the rim. He snapped the lid up and sniffed the contents, and removed the lid. Then I recoiled in disgust as Weasel Will actually drank the contents!

"Ugh!" I cried out uncontrollably. Embarrassed and ashamed as I felt my face contort into a gnarled grimace and my shoulders tense up into an unmistakable shrug of revulsion, my legs scrambled beneath me to make a mad dash for home.

While I pondered which route to take, Will raised his head and started flicking a gaze, his head tilted back slightly as one beady little eye examined me. He released the cup and it fell back into the trash can. As his little eye winked at me, his right hand reached over to his left wrist to wind his watch, then he turned toward the park and slapped his way down the sidewalk. I escaped for the safety of the storefront, safe in the knowledge that Sherm would arrive soon to belittle me on my first day of work.

*   *   *   *

My life and trials would continue and as the next few dozen years passed, a parade of street people and homeless wandered the streets of downtown Pershing. No different than anyone else, they gather wherever they can find comfort, shelter, and support, typically available in urban centers, where private enterprises, church groups, and government institutions strive to provide assistance to those in need. The survival skills of many indigents, like Weasel Will, far surpass those of us who are considered "normal" members of society. Clearly, Will's ability to take care of himself exceeded mine—of that I am certain. I have always held special regard for individuals like Will, who, for reasons usually known only unto themselves, have chosen to navigate their lives along the fringes of society.

Sometime later, in the late '90s, a brief article appeared in the *Pershing Daily News* about an elderly man who died in his sleep in a rooming house, alone, without family or known friends. The article made mention of two things—clothes and money, neither of which he lacked. Every sock, shoe, and pocket belonging to this lonesome outcast was stuffed with wads of cash, nearly a quarter-million dollars worth. There was no mention of the one true friend that had kept company with this man for twenty-some-odd-years—after all this time, the gentle, drumming tick-tick-tick of the shiny little gold watch would be silenced, the fingers that lovingly wound it now stilled.

*   *   *   *

SEEKING A SMILE

The electric motor droned with the buzz of a beehive and the ten-inch slab of steel that is the lathe chuck spun inches from my face while I dribbled oil on the cutting surface. Thin, apple-peel spirals of brass whirled off the cutting tool and fell onto a mounting pile at my feet. I had already spent an hour truing the block of metal into a smooth cylinder that would become the barrels for clock springs. With only a few millimeters to go, I thought it expedient to increase the depth of the cutter. As I turned the knob to drive it deeper, the soft whine changed to a grinding chatter and the smooth shavings transformed into coarse chips flying into my face and clicking when they hit the floor. Several hundred pounds of lathe began to chitter and vibrate. I attempted to pull the cutter back out, but I was too late. The sounds became louder until, THUD, the cutter grabbed and dove deep into the brass and sheared off, throwing the cylinder off center to crash against the tool rest.

The lathe shook violently as I jumped away from it. Just as I was certain the clanging would bring the ceiling down on us, the angry machine spit the two-pound, gouged cylinder of lethal projectile against the wall, then returned to its soft drone as I stood panting in disbelief at what I'd done.

Bill had already dropped his project and stood nearby, witnessing my foible. He should have cursed me and launched into a lecture on the mechanics of cutting metal. He could have scolded me for wasting a carefully designed cutting tool and ten dollars worth of brass. Instead, he casually walked over to flip the lathe switch off and retrieve the mangled cylinder from the floor. "Got in a hurry, eh?" he casually remarked as he examined the gouge and the dent sustained by the cylinder as it struck the unforgiving brick foundation.

"I guess," I tentatively responded, shrugging sheepishly.

"Uh, huh."

Bill walked over to a stock shelf to pull out a raw piece of tool steel for a cutter and a new block of brass. He carried them back to me, placed one in each of my hands, then cautioned, with a wry grin, "Won't do that again, will ya?"

"Nope."

"Start over," he said, his smile now as wide as his cheeks could stretch.

✳   ✳   ✳   ✳

I attended college for two years, but I had difficulty concentrating on my studies. My heart had become firmly attached to the dirty workbenches, torches, tweezers, and eccentric oldworlders of this little shop, where I returned to work at every possible opportunity.

On one particular quiet noon hour, while Bill was at lunch, I sat at his bench as I often did, trying to catch him up on some of the simple jobs I'd learned to do while watching over his shoulder. I was deep in concentration when he approached from the back room.

"Should I grunt for ya?" he caught me straining to reshape a wedding band that had found its way into a garbage disposal.

Usually, I had replaced all his tools and removed my body from his bench by the time Bill returned from his nap, but today I'd gotten carried away and lost track of the time. Startled and afraid he might be angry at my intrusion, I dropped the tools and jumped out of the chair, holding the ring behind my back as I got to my feet.

"Let's see it," he said as he looked around me for my hidden masterpiece.

With a pleading grin, I presented the ring that, although now nicely rounded, still looked like it had fought a losing battle. Bill pulled the magnifying visor down over his glasses and tumbled the ring around in his fingers, examining every square millimeter.

"Not bad," he offered, "Not bad at all. But you won't get very far like this."

For the next forty-five minutes, Bill explained that a gold ring worn for years and nicely pounded by the teeth of a garbage grinder would be hardened and tough.

Then the real lesson began. Bill bathed the ring in water, rolled it in a dish of boric acid powder to coat it, placed it on a round, asbestos pad, struck his flint, and brought his torch to life. The blue and yellow flames tickled the ring, turning the powder into a glass shield to protect the outer surfaces of the gold. Slowly, he brought the ring up to temperature until it glowed red. Then he pulled the torch back slightly to control the heat in the ring until he felt that the molecules of gold and alloy had danced enough to ease their bond, the metal softening enough to be pliable.

"The process," he instructed, "is called annealing."

Bill then allowed the ring to cool for a few minutes before "pickling" it in another type of acid to remove the glass coating and discoloration. After rinsing off the pickling solution in a soapy bath, the artistry began.

Bill pounded and filed, then applied more boric acid and more torch work. He pickled and cleaned the ring again, pounded a few more times against a steel mandrel with the familiar "CRANG-CRANG," and did some reshaping with his electric hand piece. By the time he had run the ring through the industrial-size buffing machine and given it a final cleaning, the ring looked as good as it had the day the groom slipped it on his bride's finger.

Bill then wiped the ring with a cloth before handing it to me.

"You can't even tell it was damaged," I said, amazed, as I tumbled it around in my fingers, examining every surface.

"That's the way it works when you do it right," Bill replied, pride oozing out of every pore.

"It's incredible!"

"Not so…if you know how to do it."

"I can't believe it."

"You could learn, Steve."

"Huh?"

"I've always wanted a student, and you have the knack for it."

"Gee, I dunno, Bill."

"You can do it if your heart's in it, but it would take years."

"Uh…I dunno."

"To learn the trade—the right way—you'd have to work six days a week, taking my bench on the days I'm off, and you'd have to work in my shop at home at least one evening every week."

Bill didn't get an answer that day, just the stupefied expression of a kid who traipsed through life without a clue about his future. Bill sought a student with potential, a real apprentice who could learn the trade at Bill's elbow. Such an individual would necessarily possess raw talent so considerable that, with Bill's help, he could develop into a true craftsman himself. The only talent I recognize in myself was the ability to grasp the joy in life. Fortunately, Bill perceived something more useful.

∗   ∗   ∗   ∗

Stumbling awkwardly to gain a foothold on my life's path, that summer I did, indeed, find myself working twelve to sixteen hours every day, six days each week at a future seemingly ordained by fate. Each time I wavered—and I did so more than once—some force drew me back.

Mountains of books, piles of diagrams, courses on gemology, and seven years of working side-by-side with Bill taught me the basics required to build or repair clocks, watches, and jewelry.

"Some people turn work away because they feel the value of the piece is beneath than their talent," Bill explained, emphasizing the virtue of avoiding specialization in my work. "What they fail to understand is that Grandma's three-dollar brooch probably has greater value to one person than another's thousand-dollar diamond ring. Take pride in what you do, son. The work you turn away today may be the work you're begging for tomorrow."

"What if you get too much work?"

"Better to have someone angry because you took too long to get it right rather than have someone mad because you hurried and got it wrong," Bill advised, sagely.

He smiled enthusiastically *every* time I got it wrong. He smiled a lot. He knew well that my making a mistake with him as a guide provided a far better education than accidentally getting it right.

Bill spoke occasionally of his beloved father, from whom he'd learned everything from growin' a fine ripe tomata,' to playing dentist on a horse. At the age of fifty-four, Bill's dad had fallen ill and died unexpectedly. Ever wary of the threat that heredity held over his future, Bill intended to retire at fifty-four and take a paddlewheel ride down the Mississippi.

My seventh year of watching Billy smile ended shortly after his fifty-fourth birthday. Vi made roast beef with mashed potatoes and a magnificent chocolate layer cake. We enjoyed neatly wrapped sandwiches for days.

By the time Bill's departure actually arrived, he had stopped talking about paddlewheel boats. I figured Bill had just decided to seek contentment in taking care of his son, Christopher, in comfort and enjoying an occasional thick slice of home grown sweet onion.

But I was wrong. Bill hadn't slowed down out of choice. When the chilled autumn winds ripped down on us from the north and began stripping rainbow-colored leaves from weather wearied trees, Billy fell gravely ill. On a lonesome fall morning, as Michiganders watched the vibrance of summer fade from the landscape, Bill got up from his bench and asked for someone to take him to the hospital. He never returned.

If only I could muster half the talent of my lost friend. Perhaps he made so few mistakes because he hadn't had someone to smile over him, encouraging him at every juncture. To this day, each time I err, I lift my eyes, seeking the gentle guidance of that knowing smile, and every time a suitable moment arises, I clang my mentor's mandrel proudly.

MOMENT BY MOMENT

Summer plunged upon us once again and Mick vacationed at some sunny beach while I played answering service to inquisitive women and filled in on engraving chores. One quiet afternoon, Dale handed me an inexpensive gold-plated money clip and instructed me to engrave a block "R" on it. He'd just sold it as a birthday gift, and the customer needed it the following day, so at my first opportunity I strolled into the wrapping room to set up the engraving machine. After selecting the appropriate template and securing it in position, I clamped the money clip into the vise and centered the engraving surface. After setting the seven different measurements and having tightened the seven different knobs to engrave a simple "R," I placed the stylus in the template, pressed the graver against the shiny surface, and the stylus ran smoothly through the template, transferring the image cleanly to the fresh surface. About half-way through the job, the phone rang out and the doorbell began ding-clanking, driving me to distraction.

At the very moment my attention was drawn to the unanswered phone, the stylus slid out of the confines of the template and the diamond-tipped graver slid effortlessly across the money clip. I rushed over and picked up the receiver.

"Good morning, Wynn & Scutter. How may I help you?"

"Good morning. May I speak with Mick, please?"

"I'm sorry, but Mick is not in today. Is there something I might help you with, or may I take a message?"

"No, thank you. I need to speak with Mick. Will he be in tomorrow?"

I wasn't in the mood, "He won't be back until a week from Monday. I don't know where he is, I don't know who he's with, and I don't know what he's doing."

"Oh…Thank you," click.

I hurried back to the machine and pulled the money clip from the vise. My beautiful Arabic "R" looked more like a cryptic Chinese scribble. The solution was clear—I would have to buy another one and do the engraving over again. I searched and searched our inventory, but found nothing like it. I began to perspire as the tension mounted. Surely, with all the jewelry stores in downtown Pershing, I could find another, I assured myself. I requested an early lunch after Molly returned from coffee, and my search commenced.

Clay's had nothing even remotely resembling the piece. At Lymans I got a, "sorry kid," but no match.

I explained my blunder to Mr. Pinker at his shop and showed him the savage gash.

"I need to find one just like it."

"Sorry, Steve," sympathized Mr. Pinker. "That style was discontinued over a year ago and I'm sold out. I wish I could help."

I plodded on to Brogan's…Snow's…Bush Jewelers. Nothing. I searched three men's clothing stores and every jeweler until I was down to the last one.

Finally, I stood in front of the Gem Market, beaten, depressed, and afraid I would have to return and confess my error first to Dale, then to the customer.

Show-Me-the-Cash Sonny didn't have employees, so, knowing who I would be dealing with, I prepared myself. I had twenty dollars in my wallet, mostly ones. I removed them, and, clenching them firmly in one hand, carefully adjusted them so the ends of the bills were plainly visible. Grasping the money clip in my other hand, I opened the smudged door and walked in as a bell sounded a familiar "Ding…Clank."

The Specter rested on a stool at the back of the room, his spooky posture unchanged. Even in a sitting position, he towered over everything, and now Sonny loomed over the case between us. He stood as I entered. Thin hairs, I noticed, jutted out above his ears—hat or no hat. The same fixed gaze burned into me. Petrified, I stepped forward, making sure the hand with the cash was clearly in sight.

"Mornin'," he said.

"Good morning, Mr. Markowitz," I replied politely.

"What can I help you with?" he asked, eyes glancing down at the cash in my hand as I approached. With both palms on the counter just as Mick had described him, Sonny fixed his stern gaze on me.

"I...Uhhh...I need to find something."

"What are you looking for?"

"I...Uhhh...I need to find one of these," I said, showing him the clip.

I had intended to ask to look at his money clips, but fear kept me lip-locked and I handed him the damaged piece.

As he scooped the money clip from my palm, I felt beads of sweat form on my forehead. He looked the piece over, turning it top to bottom without changing his expression. He set it on the counter, where it touched the glass with a "click," then turned and walked with a gangly stoop to a front wall case and slid the glass aside. I placed my twenty dollars on the glass next to the source of my pain.

Sonny selected a few boxes from the shelves to examine and put them back. I reached up to shuffle a five-dollar bill to the top of the stack to create a more imposing pile of money. Sonny continued to peruse the boxes until he was satisfied with his selection, then slowly, man and box hunched back to where I stood and Sonny placed it on the counter.

"I think this is what you're looking for," he said, looking first at the cash, then at me.

"Thank you," I offered, comparing the two clips. "It's close, but not just right."

My defeat overcame my fear, and no doubt it showed.

"Just a minute," he said as he looked at the cash again, taking the clip up front to trade it for another. Sonny returned and placed the new option on the case, obviously interested in the pile on the counter.

"How 'bout this?"

Salvation from embarrassment sat before me; the clips were identical.

"That's it!" I exclaimed, drifting into my own little world, oblivious to my surroundings.

I was already imagining the methodical, uninterrupted procedure of cutting a perfect Arabic "R" onto the clip. As I stared at the dusty, but new and unspoiled birthday present, Sonny's giant hand reached across the case and picked up the box, snapping the lid closed. My jaw dropped and I looked up into his leering eyes. His other great paw swooped down and snatched up the pile of cash. Jolted back to reality, I realized I was about to have my knees broken by the henchman.

Sonny gently placed the box on top of the pile of cash and his huge fist transported them over the counter to place them in my hands.

"Get it right this time, son," he said, wearily, "so it doesn't cost us any more money."

*   *   *   *

Moments coincided and lapsed one to the other until they were forgotten or blended to constitute the remnants of our lives. Sixteen years later, as I labored studiously at Bill's bench, Dale called me into his office.

"I'm retiring," he said bluntly.

"I beg your pardon?"

"I've had enough," he continued. "I'm sixty-three years old. None of us know what's ahead and I'd like to spend some time with my family. I've worked long enough to be able to live comfortably. I need to know if you want to buy the business."

The ramifications of the statement extended far beyond the obvious. Dale would retain ownership of the building, which he'd purchased only ten years earlier, and the rent would provide him with a consistent, long-term source of retirement income. The real clincher, of course, was the cost of the business itself.

South Persy had been closed years ago. Nellie wouldn't retire because even in failing health, she wouldn't leave the store to the whims of a stranger. So rather than work his own mother into the grave, Dale closed the original family business and sold the building. Giving in, Nellie moved to a comfortable retirement center where, I understand, one of the octogenarian's children was once heard to ask if someone was pumping laughing gas into the cafeteria.

The Alaidon store closed soon after, giving way to a bigger, fancier store, the kind that enabled the huge fancy mall to generate bigger fancier rents. Maggie and her husband moved to a tiny island in the Caribbean to minister to needy children.

All that remained was our quaint little shop on a nearly empty side street in downtown Pershing, nearly deserted by the retail trade. Casual discussions had touched on Dale's concern for the continuity of the business upon his retirement, but I had always assumed he would continue working well into his senior years, giving me ample time to contemplate and prepare.

This sudden turn of events was unexpected and unprecedented. There I stood, faced with the terrifying reality that the business could be mine—for the meager sum of roughly ten times my current net worth. How could I find a way to do it with barely a nickel in my pocket?

But I wasn't easily discouraged. Summoning up all my resolve to take a shot at this unexpected dream, I assembled a fancy portfolio to present the notion that I knew what I was doing. I devised a scheme in which Dale would carry the substantial portion of the note, but I would provide a substantial goodwill down-payment.

I nervously walked to my appointment at the first bank I chose, knowing full well they would courteously examine my portfolio, show me the door with consummate professionalism, then laugh like hyenas for hours once I was out of ear-shot. Weeks later I would receive a form letter thanking me for choosing their institution for my attempt at entrepreneurship. The loan officer I'd been appointed was aptly named Mr. Hatchet. Like the hanging judge, I decided he sat at his desk all day, giving the axe to every fool with a Don Quixote delusion.

As expected, upon my arrival the loan officer appeared, smiling and gracious. I handed him my portfolio of personal histories, business histories, present inventories, incomes and expenses, predicted business incomes and expenses and every other trivial fact I could scour up to document. He genuinely read every piece of paper in the folder, fingers flying so fast on a calculator they were just a blur. When he finished, a strip of paper streamed out of the calculator across his desk and fell to the floor by my feet. I painfully wondered if the numbers added up to someone who knew their stuff.

"Impressive presentation," he said, "How soon?"

"Oh, the sooner you give me an answer, the sooner I can decide what to do next."

"No, I mean how soon do you need it?"

"Huh?" I asked, doing a double-take.

"Well, this is very doable, I think. It will take me at least a week to process the paperwork, and there's a two-hundred and fifty dollar processing fee. But we can take care of that at closing."

"Huh?" I repeated, dumbfounded.

"You didn't think this possible, did you?"

"Well…uhh…no, at least not this easily."

"The business certainly has been around long enough, and according to this paperwork, it remains stable. The real key here is your longevity; you've been at your job about four times as long as I've been at mine. As far as the bank is concerned, you have substantial equity in your home, and that's what we'll use. Some cash for working capital is usually one of our requirements, but we'll work around that."

Dale may have had more confidence in my financial capabilities than I, or maybe not. In any event, one month later we walked the three blocks back to the shop from the law offices where all the papers were signed. We laughed and reminisced, strolling through a changed downtown, with our wives at our sides, one woman profoundly proud of her husband's accomplishments, the other profoundly fearful of what hers had wrought.

Most of downtown Pershing's shops and all of the department stores had gone. Only three of the eighteen jewelry stores I knew all those years ago remained, and one was on precarious ground. Our shadows reflected from the windows of empty storefronts, climbing the lonely exteriors of bricked-up office buildings.

We waltzed through the door of our little shop, the familiar old "Ding...clank" of the brass bell replaced now by a sterile, electronic "Ding...dong" at the back of the showroom. My daytime family labored at their benches and behind the cases, and a few customers ambled about the room, admiring beautiful possibilities behind the glass.

Dale drifted among the ranks from bench to desk, thanking everyone for his or her loyal service and support. We met up again in his office, which had been the wrapping room in the old days. The cash register remained at its old station, one of the hundred assets I had overlooked. Dale punched the key to open the cash drawer, instantly snapping me out of the euphoric state clouding my mind.

I had a moment of déjà vu when I found myself unable to find enough money in my pocket to buy a cup of coffee. Jeanne, my wife of only a few years, and I had confirmed the balance in our checking account that morning, and I could still see the spindly numbers wobbling in the ledger; the balance column read "thirty-one dollars and twelve cents." And I hadn't deducted the previous month's service charges yet...

Dale must have sensed my anxiety, because he hesitated over the drawer. "I'm going to start you out with your first till," he said, counting out fifty dollars in ones and fives, placing them in the appropriate slots, and flipping the spring-loaded levers to hold them in place. "You're going to be just fine," he said, then he shook my hand and left.

*   *   *   *

With the addition of the coins already in the cash drawer, we began our life as business owners with about sixty dollars in small change. Miraculously, it grew. It grew into hundreds, enabling us to pay the first week's payroll. It grew into thousands and tens of thousands, so we could pay rent and note payments, purchase merchandise, parts, and materials, pay contract labor, accounting fees, and buy more checks.

A few short weeks after the transition, though, our newer aluminum and plastic cash register froze up and died, so we tossed it out with the leftover French fries and junk mail. We replaced it with a fancier, sleeker, even more plastic version that would last only three years.

Running a small business is indeed like child's play. It's a board game of buying and selling and collecting fines and fees. The little paper bills multiply into huge stacks of cash on your side of the table until you land on someone else's space and hand it to them in great gobs. Often times you roll the die from sweaty palms, staring at the last little denomination tucked under the board at your place. Hopes and dreams require the cube to make a fortuitous landing and tease you into continuing the game tomorrow.

Months pass and delusions of grandeur battle in your brain against the possibilities of failure. Consumed by the demands of the business, your life begins to tick away like minutes and you roll the die, roll the die. You rely on every experience and lean on every quirky idea to gain an edge, and yet the piles of money dwindle faster than they grow until a lucky roll brings you back to do it again.

$$* \qquad * \qquad * \qquad *$$

Jeanne and I decided to take a break on a lovely Friday evening that summer. We enjoyed a rare relaxing dinner with wine and dancing, savoring the music of our favorite local entertainer. It was the perfect kind of evening couples should experience regularly, but do so rarely. The world begins to slow, and moments become part of your reality again. Tensions flee when shared glances and tender words reveal the depths once discovered, but which are nearly buried in the turmoil of modern life.

During the long drive home, we listened to soft music on the radio and vowed to one another we would never let so much time pass before we did this again. Full of wine and pleasant thoughts, Jeanne rested her head on my shoulder and drifted into a peaceful reverie. To keep myself from joining her before we reached home safely, I changed the radio to a local news-and-talk program. The announcer's words burst sharply into my world, burning a new space onto the game board.

"The firefighters are smashing through the windows of the old building just above the jewelry store!" the announcer sputtered. "Smoke is billowing everywhere and it's difficult to see, but flames are rocketing thirty feet above the roof, Jack!"

"Paul, does it look like they can contain the fire?"

"No. No—the building's going up fast. I've never seen anything like it!" the announcer shouted loudly, out of breath, trying to carry over the sounds of sirens and horns. "The ladders are backing away from the building now. The whole thing's like a bomb exploding, Jack! you just can't believe it!"

"Paul, can they contain the fire? Is it going to spread to other buildings downtown?"

Every word stabbed, pierced and twisted in my heart. I listened intently.

Which store—was there any sign of which store it was? Which building? What block, for God's sakes? I dreaded the answer to the questions ripping away at me, but I needed to know the answers.

Jeanne wriggled uncomfortably on my now-rigid shoulder. *Why wake her?* I reasoned. She'll know the bad news soon enough. The car steered itself toward downtown. There seemed to be no other road to travel. From a mile away, the heavy black smoke clouded the sky and a nauseating orange glow radiated up into the darkness. Tears filled my eyes, causing the glow to blur against the skyline. Flickering white and red lights danced on distant upper windows as we neared the city center. As the flashing lights of police cars rudely woke Jeanne from her rest, I wished she could have stayed safe in her dream. As she shook off the drunkenness of sleep, she thought I'd been pulled over for speeding.

"It's O. K." I said. "A building is on fire downtown. Nobody's hurt, but I want to check on the store. You wait here and go back to sleep."

Before I could even get out of the car, Jeanne was halfway down the block, purse banging against her hip. The woman I married wouldn't have shed so much as a tear had I lost all of our earthly possessions, simply because she values other things more highly.

As we approached the crowds of gawking bystanders protected behind police barricades, we could see that several hundred feet from Wynn & Scutter, the Gem Market was already a burning corpse of a building, its roof and upper floors collapsing in torrents of flame and noxious fumes.

I looked over the crowds to see a group of police officers, dwarfed by a familiar, stooping giant. As Sonny gazed at the smoldering memories that were his, I could see the firelight dance from the wetness on his cheeks. I wanted to run over and put my arm around him and say, "I guess we didn't get it right this time," only I felt it best to let him stand over this pyre alone. I knew the kind of memories he was burying that night—there would be millions of them, and they would be his greatest solace.

I never thanked Sonny—not really. Sure, a quirky eighteen-year-old kid gave him a fleeting, "Gee, thanks" for saving him from humiliation, and I did start waving, smiling, and saying "hello" whenever I caught him looming down the sidewalk, but I never walked up to him and said, "Mr. Markowitz, I'd like to thank you for the generous and gracious kindness you bestowed on a confused and frightened child."

Sadly, Sonny died several months after the fire from an emotional wound that could not heal. It is said the only thing recovered from the pile of ashes was a charred little metal box, and that he held it close to him when he left downtown for the last time. I wonder what treasure was sealed in that blackened box—a pile of cash, perhaps? A bundle of diamond and gemstone parcels, maybe? Or possibly something like my own tarnished, gold-plated money clip with a cryptic Chinese scribble gouged permanently onto the surface…

*   *   *   *

JILTED WOMEN AND
JEWEL THIEVES

I had just completed the morning bookkeeping, adding the previous day's business to the ledger and hoping that someday in the not-too-distant future, a calculator would be required to tabulate the figures. I stepped out of the office adjacent to the showroom to see which bird was after the worm this morning.

A doorbell has been virtually useless since the bakery moved in next door a few years ago. They heat up their massive ovens at one o'clock in the morning, so we've had to prop the door open most days, even in the winter, to help release the second-hand wet heat into the street. No matter—the sweet and friendly "ding…clank" I enjoyed for so many years has since been replaced by the sterile "ding…dong" of a supposedly more efficient electronic sensor.

I looked over at Marv—his elbows propped on the counter top, his binocular-type lens turned down in front of his eyeglasses to examine a repair for the first customer of the day—I thought back to the first time we met. It was summer break during college. The time moved quickly—I'd already experienced a month of browbeating courtesy of Sherm—and I had already gathered and tossed a hefty load of dried-up peanut butter sandwiches.

A very young looking fellow stopped in and requested an audience with Dale. After chatting for half an hour or so, Dale brought him around back and introduced him to the crew, all hard at work. I should have pegged the fellow as a watchmaker at first glance; the dead giveaway was the stern, forthright nature that never allowed him to waste a smile during the introductions, but I didn't catch it. With a boyish appearance accentuated by his abbreviated height—a mere nudge over five feet—the young man couldn't have been out of his teens yet.

"Marvin is a watchmaker, you guys, and he'll be working with Sherm to help with the work load."

As Mick, Molly, Bill, and I smiled a hearty welcome, Sherm sort of winced and hunched back into his work. When Marvin shrugged our smiles off with what seemed to be a horologist's typical stoic nature, I knew he would be perfect for the job. From what I could see, some kind of "happiness lobotomy" seemed to be a prerequisite to watchmaker training.

Marv fit in perfectly. He joined our merry band to learn the ornery but noble ways of Sherm, just as Sarah learned from Molly, Jill learned from Mick, and I learned from Bill and Dale. Together we would constitute a younger troupe of eccentric souls practicing old-world geezerdom in a more modern form—and we would be almost as good at it.

Each of us brought our own personal strengths to compensate for whatever wisdom we had failed to absorb from our mentors. Take me, for instance; while I lacked even the most minuscule iota of business savvy, I more than made up for it with my abundant supply of pure dumb luck, which had carried us this far and managed to keep Dale jabbing anvil-ended sticks at little white balls outside of his condo somewhere in the Carolinas.

The electric "ding-dong" jolted me back to the here and now as Bernice and Eunice made their way into the shop. One of the most heartwarming benefits of working in a small business is greeting familiar, friendly old faces. They become like family, and they're always welcome.

"Good morning, Eunice. Good morning, Bernice. It's so nice to see you," I said, happy to see the twins.

Deep in conversation, the ladies were likely reminiscing about old downtown Pershing, as everyone who dropped in seemed to do. A broad smile perked up beneath Eunice's sparkly eyes as she turned to look at me; while still discontent with her lot in life, Bernice's deeply creased frown lines won the fight as she tried to fake a grin.

We exchanged our usual pleasantries, spoke of the weather, and remembered a few of the stores that used to be part of our beautiful downtown. With Molly gone and no coffee to gossip over, we slipped into our comfortable routine—making an event out of admiring all the merchandise in the store. We played point and place; they would point at an item and I would place it on the counter. They'd point again, and I'd put the old one back in its place, then pull out the next one. Amazingly, this is the way many people passed the day, sometimes for hours.

At some point during our charade, the store invariably began to fill with real shoppers—downtown workers on their break. Oblivious to the "paying" customers, Bernice would point out how inferior the necklace on the counter was compared to that around her neck, which she occasionally fingered while sharing a little anecdote about the trip to Italy during which she'd purchased it.

Bernice's necklace could have been beautiful—if she'd cleaned it occasionally. I cringed every time she pointed to it, because the once-attractive, hand-woven eighteen-karat-gold piece was plastered with gluey hair spray, which in turn attracted dust like a magnet. I noticed that this finely crafted gold looked no more elegant now than her cheap costume pieces she'd worn twenty-five years before.

The store filled with customers who, on tight schedules, eyeballed us with increasing impatience, so I thought it best to break the monotony of the imaginary shopping spree and offered to check the sisters' rings for them.

Agreeable, Eunice said, "Oh, yes, I haven't had these looked at in such a long time. Could you clean them, too?" She smiled as she removed the rings from her fingers and handed them to me.

"Of course," I replied, "I'd be deligh…"

"Mine too," Bernice broke in, yanking rings from her fingers and dropping them on the glass counter, clack…clack…clack. Hers was not a request or even a suggestion, but a demand. Her harsh gaze, I now realized, reflected the deep-seated unhappiness she had harbored since discovering her husband's infidelity twenty years ago and then divorcing him. Poor Bernice! Forever scarred by her husband's misdeeds, she harbored a lifelong disdain for the entire male gender.

"And my necklace, too. It could use a good cleaning," Bernice added, brusquely, dropping it. The piece crashed onto the counter like an anchor chain slamming into a plate glass window.

As my three co-workers scurried to handle the crowd of people gathering on the showroom floor, I hustled to the back of the shop where our cleaning equipment was located. After hanging the rings on a rack in our ultrasonic machine, I placed the necklace across the top of the hangers and flipped the switch. There was so much debris enmeshed in the half-inch woven gold that as it loosened and fell away, it appeared as though I'd poured black ink into the transparent cleaning solution.

I waited until I was certain the industrial grade, peel-the-skin-off-your-fingers cleaning solution container was thoroughly filled with gook, then dumped it out. I mixed another batch and finished cleaning and steaming the rings with our high pressure cleaner before setting the necklace back in the clear solution. More inky goo appeared.

As I returned to the showroom, which was now filled by an even larger mob of impatient customers, I checked the condition of the rings as I handed them back to the sisters.

"Where's my necklace?" demanded Bernice.

"It needed some additional cleaning due to its tight, heavy weave, so I left it a little longer."

"I want my necklace—now! Where is it?" she asked insistently.

"I'll get it right away," I said politely, my patience taxed.

Upon returning to the cleaning machine, I had to use a pair of forceps to fish around in the new batch of inky black liquid. I grasped and extricated an amazingly beautiful handcrafted neckpiece, exhibiting the luster and gleam it had been designed to radiate. I steamed the necklace, patted it dry admiringly, ran it gently through a rouge cloth to enhance its warm glow, then returned and placed the beautiful piece of craftsmanship on a black velvet pad in front of the twins. Eunice smiled. Bernice looked down, frowned, then glared at me.

"What's this cheap piece of junk?" she whined, anger searing the air between us. "This isn't my necklace!"

Amazed and somewhat shaken, it took me a moment to regain my composure. "Of course it is, Bernice. It's just cleaner!"

"Take this away! It's gaudy-looking junk! Where's my expensive necklace?" Bernice's eyes burned into me as she screamed, accusingly, "You've stolen it!"

From every corner of the showroom, wide-eyed customers gazed at me, the "crook" behind the counter. A few, with their little envelopes and plastic bags of broken jewelry in hand, headed immediately for the door.

Eunice's face grew pasty as she slowly took a step away from her sister. "Bernice, I think you'd better take a closer look. It might be yours."

"It most certainly is not!" exclaimed Bernice. "He's taken mine out back and switched it for this cheap piece of junk!"

"Bernice," I pleaded, "look at it closely. This is the same delicate weave." I lifted the chain from the velvet pad. "Feel the weight and look at the stamp on the tag near the clasp." I took an eye loupe from my pocket and mimicked its use. "Right here," I said, pointing to the tag, "it says 'Italy 750'—you can see it plain as day." I handed the loupe to Bernice.

"Seven-fifty. What's seven-fifty? My necklace is eighteen karat, not this junk."

Throughout the ordeal, my loyal coworkers attempted to continue the business at hand, while only a few familiar faces remained as more customers fled the shop. No one said a word as the crowd thinned out. You could have heard a pin drop. All ears were bent in our direction, all eyes watched with sidelong glances.

"Seven-five-zero," I explained to Bernice, "is the European quality stamp for eighteen karat gold. It means that seven hundred and fifty parts per thousand, or seventy-five percent of the metal content is gold…same as the American eighteen karat symbol."

"You can't fool me with your thieving ways," Bernice snapped through an evil sneer, scaring a new customer right out of the shop.

"I wouldn't steal your jewelry, Mrs. Walker," I objected. "We've known each other for a very long time. You don't really believe I'd do such a thing, do you?"

"You go back, reach into whatever hole you've hidden my necklace in, and give it back!" she shrieked.

I could not allow this to continue. In addition to the direct loss of at least a half-dozen customers, Bernice's assault on my reputation would create a domino effect, extending to their coworkers, families, friends, and even passing acquaintances. Within a short time the legend of the "jewel thief of Pershing" would reach hundreds of people.

"Mrs. Walker, I'm going to have to ask you to take your necklace and leave my store," I said quietly but firmly, confident that the sisters' next stop would be at the nearest competing jeweler, who would confirm my claims.

"I think that's a good idea. Let's take it and go," agreed Eunice.

"I'm not leaving without my expensive necklace!" Bernice growled, her eyes burning a hole right through me.

"Mrs. Walker, you are making false accusations here. What I am telling you is true, and the truth is the only defense I need. I'm afraid you're going to have to leave now, as I cannot allow you to chase any more of my customers out of the store. I encourage you to take this to another jeweler. If you want my guarantee in writing, I'll give it to you right now to take along."

"Yes, Bernice, let's go. Take the necklace and we'll go some place else," Eunice prodded, clearly aware of and embarrassed by her sister's folly.

"It's a shame that they ever let you in here," Bernice snarled at me, snatching the necklace from the velvet pad, "this used to be a nice place, with nice people. I'll be back to get you, young man. I'll teach you what comes of your thieving ways!"

The sisters turned and walked out the door, leaving me flustered, angry, and humiliated all at once. Shaken, I had never before asked anyone to leave the shop. If I'd paid Nostradamus himself to predict my future and he'd told me I would be ejecting a customer—an elderly woman I'd known for over twenty years—I would have demanded my money back for his incompetence. What really bothered me the most, however, was that Bernice could even entertain the notion that I might be such a low-life worm.

After the sisters left, the only sound in the room came from the little radio, softly spouting an old Nat King Cole tune about love and promise and trust. To find some privacy, I had to walk past Sarah and a young customer shopping for an engagement ring.

"Bob, here, has a couple of questions you can answer better than me," Sarah said, softly, gently stopping me before I could go in back to sulk.

"Oh, uh, sure," I stammered, "of course. What have we come up with, Bob? How can I help you?"

"Was she for real?" Bob wondered in amazement. "Does that stuff happen all the time?"

"Unfortunately, you're too young to know yet, but things like that happen to all of us in one way or another from time to time."

"What a rude old biddy."

"Don't hold it against her, Bob. For whatever reason, she really believes I could be that low."

"You didn't really switch her chain, did you?"

"Certainly not. I cleaned it and it looked different. She's managed to develop and fertilize a strong mistrust of certain people."

"Glad I'm not marrying a woman like that. Can you even imagine?"

"Bob…you *are* marrying a woman like that, and your bride will be marrying a man like that."

"No way, man!"

"Of course you are. I knew Bernice when she thought she was happily married. She was a different person. When she got shafted by a scoundrel of a husband, her life changed; she changed. You're making a much larger decision today than just selecting a diamond; this is only where it begins. Where you and your bride take it from here will determine who and what you are and will be for the rest of your life. Right now, you're just worried about how to spend a few hundred dollars, but there's a great deal more at stake than you realize. There use to be a jeweler down the street who'd tell you, as part of his sales pitch, 'If you buy your diamond from me, I'll dance at your wedding.' Well, if you buy your diamond from me, I'd rather dance at your fiftieth anniversary. That way I'll know you made the right choices along the way, and you've had a happy life."

"I'll take this one," Bob said, pensively.

"Good choice. I'll try to live long enough to have a dance with your bride on your golden anniversary."

*   *   *   *

Four months later, I'd just finished explaining the whys and wherefores of diamond grading to another young customer, when Bernice stepped in our door. I quickly excused myself and turned the gentleman over to Sarah, now my right hand person.

"Hello, Bernice."

"Hello, Steve."

"How may I help you this morning?" I said, pleasantly, bracing myself.

"Don't you miss Clay's? I always bought everything I needed from that department store."

"I know, we all did. You and Molly sure spent enough time in their coffee shop, too."

We smiled together at the memory.

"Eunice and I are moving to Florida. We're tired of driving in the snow."

"I think that's splendid. You're right, of course. It should be much easier to get about in year-round summer. But won't you miss the beauty of winter?"

"When you get older, you'll understand. When I get up in the morning and look out the window at fresh snow, I don't see pretty white stuff any more; all I see is another missed hair appointment."

We smiled together again.

"What can I do for you this morning, Bernice?"

"Oh, I have a pair of earrings that pinch my ears. I was hoping you'd loosen them a little for me."

Bernice had never had her ears pierced. I took the set of inexpensive costume earrings to my bench and tweaked the spring-loaded levers so they wouldn't be too tight. When I returned to the showroom floor and handed the earrings to her over the counter, she tried them on and grinned her approval.

"Thank you," she said, "they're perfect."

"Can I do anything else for you?"

"Thank you, no. Eunice is waiting in the car, so I'd better hurry." She put her hand to her neck as if to touch the necklace we'd had our tiff over, but it wasn't there.

"I know Florida is a wonderful place, and I wish you both the best of luck. If you ever miss it, though, the snow will be here every winter for you."

"I know," she said, shivering at the very thought. "Good-bye, Steve," she said gently, then turned and walked out the door.

It never fails, but when a long-standing customer graces our doorstep I can't help but remember them as they were when we first met. We all change. Those of us behind the showcases certainly have reshaped our images. We use to scurry busily behind and between the cases; now we slowly turn sideways to pass one another. Damned cinnamon rolls!

As she left my shop for the last time, I imagined the old Bernice, hoping that someday the frown lines in her cheeks and forehead would soften. Anger steals beauty from everything. Spreading like a dreaded airborne disease, anger affects everyone it touches. In a few short minutes during the necklace incident, the plague touched at least a dozen people and likely spread for miles.

Over the years, I acquired some of my most cherished friends across the shiny glass of a jewelry case. Unlike bartenders, who often hear only about their customer's troubles, I also had the opportunity to marvel at the magical lives many people build together, living out scenarios often reserved for the fairy tale books. People marry and remain together for a multitude of reasons, but as a jeweler, I have watched and admired numerous couples live and grow together in binding unions that thrived on absolutely no resources other than their passion for one another.

I've watched these relationships mature and blossom into dazzling bouquets of treasures until the inevitable day when one partner is left without the other. I have witnessed scholars and corporate chiefs, physicians and lawyers, some of the most capable, logical minds in our midst become emotional cripples at the loss of a spouse. Some recover and rediscover the joy in life, some merely find contentment, and the remainder strive to navigate the world, burdened by unyielding emptiness.

The necklace experience raised a little defensive shield in my subconscious, the kind we all develop from experience. Unfortunately, such barriers affect the way we conduct ourselves in our relationships with strangers and loved ones. Much like a Venetian blind, we have to pull the cord to raise the barrier and allow the sun to shine through, but if the mechanism has been damaged in any way the blinds can drop if we turn our backs.

They're gone now. All the old-timers are gone—Bill, Sonny, Nellie, Jody, Sherm, and Molly. Mick packed up, moved west, started his own business, and finally got married. She must be some woman.

The clock on the back wall of the shop ticks away the moments, and the memories glow off the polished swinging pendulum. There is a different group of us now—newer, faster, and almost as good. We learned from the oldworlders, and we do it their way. Their way is best. They were always the most brilliant and most fabulous jewels that ever passed over the doorstep of this little shop.

Whenever we speak, you'll notice I always have that cord tied around my little finger to keep that shade securely open. I don't want to miss a thing. Maybe I'll rent a forklift to bring the old cash register out of the dusty back room and everything will be just fine.

0-595-32112-7

Printed in the United States
20706LVS00007B/226-261